Saint Michael's Gold

By

H. Bedford-Jones

G. P. Putnam's Sons

New York   London

The Knickerbocker Press

1926

THIS BOOK IS INSCRIBED

TO

DAVID MURRAY COWIE

WHOSE FRIENDSHIP IS HAPPILY

ABOVE CRITICISM

CONTENTS

v

CONTENTS

SAINT MICHAEL'S GOLD

SAINT MICHAEL'S GOLD

CHAPTER I

LIBERTY AND EQUALITY, IF NOT FRATERNITY

L AST days in Paris are always eventful, but
mine were to be more eventful than most.
I knew it when I wakened, at a late hour,
and found the curt note from Laurent Basse
telling of my denunciation. "See Robespierre at
once and block an arrest," he wrote. "Meet me at
five this afternoon at the Bonnet Rouge."

A glance at the clock and I was out of bed, cursing my heavy slumber. However, there was some
excuse for my eight hours of exhausted sleep, the
first in two days, and I had the satisfaction of knowing that three more women owed their lives to me.
I had been too long under the shadow of denuncia-

tion to worry over possible arrest. Ever since we voted against the king's death, Paine and the rest of us had been in the same boat.

I hurried. I had to eat, shave and dress, then stuff my few belongings into my pockets and settle up my bill for lodgings, since there would be no return here. All this behind me, I hastened out to the street. The Rue du Bac showed its usual crawling line of hackney coaches, and I beckoned one. It was past noon of Monday, the twentieth of May— a day I was to remember for its furious happenings. The morrow would be exactly four months since Louis XVI lost his head, in January of this year, 1793.

From somewhere came darting a street gamin. He flung a sharp cry at me and in passing thrust a folded newspaper into my hand; then he ran on without waiting for his money. I pocketed the paper impatiently as the hackney drew up.

"To the Tuileries—the convention hall," I said. The driver shrugged amiably.

"It will cost you five hundred francs, citizen!"

"I'll give you six hundred for speed."

"Bah!" he rejoined, with a laugh and a flourish of his whip. "Why worry over speed, citizen, when to-morrow may see you dead?"

LIBERTY AND EQUALITY

I smiled and climbed in, and the vehicle lumbered off. My smile quickly died into rueful gravity—in this saucy repartee was too much ghastly truth. Recalling the folded paper shoved into my hand, I opened it to find the latest copy of Marat's news-sheet, the "Friend of the People." Scrawled across the top of it was an unsigned message:

"Advance the hour to three. Imperative."

I shredded this into fragments and cast it away. From Laurent Basse, then—porter and proof-runner of the paper, body-guard and sole confidant of the terrible Marat. Why had he changed the rendezvous to an earlier hour? The answer was ominously simple.

"Something more has happened," I reflected, staring at the passing buildings with unseeing gaze. "If Marat has learned the truth, I'm lost. My one hope lies in Robespierre, and also in Danton; both hate and fear Marat. However, since Marat denounced me last night, he must have cause. Some spy has found me out."

The city was one of ravening wolves fast turning upon each other. The wholesale massacres of the Terror were foreshadowed. Paris, with part of France aiding her, was fighting all Europe and doing it badly at the moment. Outside Paris, the country

5

was divided into two factions, the republicans and royalists, or Blues and Whites. Inside the city were a dozen factions, tearing at each other's throats, fighting for power.

Only a fool cherishes illusions, and I had none whatever. My usefulness here was ended. It was only a matter of hours to my arrest—to-night at latest. Then I heard my name called, and something of a shock came over me.

"Martin! Citizen Martin!"

My coachman halted. Striding up from the curb was a tall alert figure only too well known to me. Clad in the most approved revolutionary fashion, even to the blue "tyrant" waistcoat and the liberty-cap pin at the neck of his shirt, this man none the less achieved a certain elegance in his appearance. Citizen Rabaut, informer, spy, betrayer of his own caste, dreaded agent of the Committee of Public Safety, had once been the Marquis de Saint-Servaut. Where others had turned coat from sincere belief, he had done so for his own advantage. I knew him for opportunist pure and simple, a man with no sincerity in anything, no respect for anyone, utterly callous. He had all the vices of the old noblesse, and none of their virtues except courage.

"So we ride together, Martin?" he exclaimed.

6

LIBERTY AND EQUALITY

At his smile, I lost my quick fear. He had not come to arrest me then.

"To what ride do you refer—one in a green cart, like the late Citizen Capet?"

He laughed easily. He was a handsome man and would go far, with his absolute lack of scruple.

"Not yet, I hope! I refer to your appointment—Laurent Basse told me of it half an hour ago. I'm glad we have met, for the business is rather urgent and secret," and he flung a glance at my driver. "By the way, I've heard rumors about you—eh? How your commission was signed, I don't know. Perhaps you'd like to get out of Paris before it's revoked—eh?"

He had a habit of saying things in this way, with a half-inquiring word at the end. His dark, insolent eyes laughed knowingly at me. I had sense enough to give him a quiet nod and not reveal my utter bewilderment at his words, for the name of Laurent Basse showed me what was afoot.

"Since we're to be companions," I responded, "we might as well get away while we can. I'm quite at your service."

"Faith, you take it carelessly!" Rabaut looked hard at me, his powerful, cleanly cut features half

7

suspicious. "Do you understand that full powers are accorded me, and nearly the same to you? I am, in fact, a commissioner—that is to say, a king. I'm to keep my eye on the procureur Fromond, who is nominally to have charge of the job." He had lowered his voice and stood beside me. "You'll get half a troop of horse at Avranches, if you want them, and will keep your eye on me. Who the devil will keep an eye on you, remains to be seen!"

He finished with a sardonic laugh. Staggered by all this, utterly at a loss, I temporized and did not dare show my abysmal ignorance of the whole matter.

"When do we leave, then, and from where?" I demanded.

He produced a gold snuffbox and sniffed the brown dust with an air.

"Basse told me of a pair of excellent horses, and I'm on my way to find and requisition them," he responded. "I suppose we'd best go by way of Versailles to Alençon, then on to Avranches. Getting safely to the coast and back will be matter for miracle—the whole country down there is an ambuscade for Blues! I'm trusting your head to work on the matter. Shall we say four-thirty this afternoon, at my lodgings—eh? You know the place, above the

LIBERTY AND EQUALITY

Café Perron in the Rue Dominique. That'll get us out of town to-night."

"Agreed," I said. "It's past noon already. Four-thirty, eh? You and I go alone?"

He nodded and stepped back, and my coach went on.

I was acutely relieved, and tried to resolve my bewilderment into some semblance of order. Obviously Laurent Basse, the porter and servant of Marat, had cooked up some scheme to get me out of Paris.

Rabaut I knew for a most unprincipled scoundrel, a man even more dreaded than Marat, eager to rise by the betrayal of anyone. He had sent his own uncle to the guillotine, and had fabricated more than one conspiracy to rescue the boy king or the queen, only to gather in his companions and send them to the knife. Fortunately, he had no suspicion that I was doomed.

This man a commissioner! Were the fact true, Rabaut would be actually more powerful than any man in France, outside Paris. The commissioners appointed by the Committee of Public Safety answered only to this central committee. Generals obeyed them. They had power over everything and everyone.

9

SAINT MICHAEL'S GOLD

"Apparently I'm something of the same sort," was my comforting reflection. "Some affair of huge size is in the wind—what the deuce can it be? Well, no matter if Rabaut doesn't learn the truth about me before four-thirty this afternoon! I'll have to wait until I meet Basse, and meantime guard my tongue."

An excellent resolution, had I been able to keep it.

Upon approaching the disorderly mass of buildings, once the Tuileries palace, it became evident I was not too late—the session had been delayed, other representatives were still arriving. The buildings roared with voices and crowds fought at the doors. My driver got his six hundred francs in fresh paper assignats, and was still grumbling when I turned away.

There were some advantages in being a representative, for I was recognized and passed by the guards with some jest, and so gained the Terrace des Feuillants. From this terrace a door reserved for members opened directly into the convention hall.

As I stepped through it into the obscurity, a hand fell upon my wrist.

For an instant I could see nothing. Outside, the day was cloudy and dark; inside it was more than dark—it was ominous. Once the royal theater, this great hall was now blurred and heavy with scaffolding and beams, dim with feeble lamps, gloomy and threatening, all disproportionate with the huge busts and statues stuck around. The only gay thing in the place was the group of immense flags above the speaker's tribune, and now even these were but vaguely visible. The session was not yet sitting, nor would be soon. Around was all the usual turbulent, cursing, shouting throng, voices storming in mad vehemence—and in my ear honest English speech, clear cut and sharp.

"Martin! This is madness, John, madness!"

Before me appeared the gentle, shrewd-eyed face of Thomas Paine. He had been waiting here, probably for me, perhaps for others. Like me, he had been given a seat in the convention as an expert revolutionist, in which science indeed he was more famed than I. My own seat came from the influence of Lafayette.

"You should not have come here," he went on rapidly. "You don't know what took place in last night's session—Marat denounced you under the decree proposed by Osselin."

"I know."

None the less this showed what I had not known—

SAINT MICHAEL'S GOLD

I was surely doomed. This terrible decree condemned to death any émigré or banished noble who returned to France, any person who tried to leave France, anyone who helped in the departure or return or who gave asylum to any such fugitive. It was this decree which was to inaugurate the Terror.

"Where've you been the past two days, man?" snapped Paine. "I've tried to reach you, but you weren't at home—"

"I've been helping three poor women out of this accursed city," I said.

Paine groaned. "Then it's true! Fournier spoke with me half an hour ago; he says Marat wants your head, Robespierre is silent, Danton frowns. If you're seen here to-day, you're lost! Get out, John, get out of here at once."

Sight of the man steadied me—he was one sane man in this convention gone mad with blood and power! That we Americans should be members here was not strange, nor were we the only ones. There was Fournier, friend of Lafayette; indeed, Washington himself had been made a member, and several English liberals.

"No," I told him. "I'm here because it's the safest place for the day. Denunciation doesn't mean arrest. They'd not arrest me here, in any case."

LIBERTY AND EQUALITY

"But to-night—"

"I'll be gone," I said, unhurried. "I've left my lodgings already. You know Marat's watch-dog, as they call him—that fellow Laurent Basse? He's heavily in my debt and is making some plan to get me out of Paris."

"You have a chance, then," and Paine looked relieved. "Is there anything I can do?"

"Yes. Don't get mixed up in my fate."

He laughed curtly. "No matter, John. They're only waiting now for some pretext to get me— Danton tipped me off yesterday. I've sent him a letter on the tumultuous misconduct of things here, and its publication may effect something—one way or the other."

"You!" I exclaimed. "They'd not dare attack you, Paine!"

"They dare anything," he said gloomily. "Danton means to bring the queen to the knife, and Marat is laying traps for Robespierre. Dare! They've gone mad, John, and you'd better get out of the madhouse."

A throng shoved into us and swept us apart.

I went on, slowly working a devious way through the wild tumult, half convinced that I had better get out yet stubbornly resisting the conviction. Sabres, pistols, knives were everywhere, threats filled the air. The Girondins, already doomed, were frantically accusing their opponents. Every man's hand was against that of every other man. Oaths and shouted imprecations were roared on all sides. If it were not so frightful, it would have been ludicrous.

I got across the floor, beneath the black-framed Declaration of the Rights of Man. An ugly place, this; the very memory of those nineteen semi-circular benches fronting the speaker's rostrum, the bare tribunes thronged with people, the gloomy, blood-spattered wood all around was unpleasantly suggestive.

This month saw the beginning of the fratricidal struggle. Paris ruled France with a throttling grip, and this convention of ours still ruled Paris; three men, Marat, Danton and Robespierre, ruled the convention. These three, already in a death-grapple, were hurling doom at all around them. And now, in the gloomy murk of this ominous hall, under the ironical statue of Liberty with Franklin's medallion affixed to her crown, I was destined to meet each of these three men, with no great luck from the encounters.

While making my way along the dark passage

14

between the benches, I suddenly collided with a tall figure, getting a sharp rap on the head.

"Pardon," I exclaimed. "Ah, Danton! I was looking for you—"

"It is not Danton," said a bitter voice, instantly apprising me of my frightful error. "Useless to seek my pardon, Citizen Martin."

The cold features of Robespierre grew before me. This man would never forgive being mistaken for Danton—his fingers were already itching for that burly throat. At his tone, anger swept through me, and I snapped at him with deliberate insult.

"Your pardon? Not at all. Rather, I should ask the pardon of Danton."

Even in the gloom, one could see how he went white at the words.

"Another song to-morrow, citizen," he answered coldly, and went his way.

There was one hope gone; with a shrug, I continued my course. Robespierre had held his peace about me, but this issue was now decided, my fate sealed by the error I had made. This man who had killed a king was inexorable and pitiless, his dark, thin shadow already projected by the red torch of the coming terror.

"There remains Danton," I thought. "He may

15

be glad to stand by me, if only to snarl at Robespierre and Marat. Danton has the army and half Paris at his back, too! If he can stave off any talk of arrest for to-day, then to-morrow I'll be gone."

I soon found where Danton stood, in this respect.

CHAPTER II

TWO figures blocked my way, one of them vehemently and furiously shouting, the other retorting with calm and deadly accusations. The first was burly, leonine, unkempt; the second, young and handsome, a terrible brooding melancholy in his eyes, a noble who had espoused the cause of liberty and had found it only a hollow mockery.

Their dispute passed unheeded by the throngs all around, since everyone was denouncing, threatening, clamoring for the next man's blood. France was gripped by men seeking wildly to keep their own feet from mounting the scaffold, yet few of them managed it. Most of the men gathered in this gloomy theater of the revolution were already death marked.

"I tell you," roared the leonine Danton, shaking

17

his heavy fist, "I tell you it is sheer folly! There is no trouble worth the name in Brittany or the Vendée—the menace to the republic comes from the frontier! Saint-Just, you talk too much and think too little."

"And you think not at all," retorted the acid-voice of Saint-Just. "You fear Prussia, but you forget yourself, Danton. Who thieved the crown jewels? Who led an army into Belgium and filled pockets like a common robber? Who stole the hundred thousand pounds of the Ministry of Justice?"

"Ask, you ci-devant dog!" howled Danton, almost stifled by an access of rage. "If Santerre rolled drums to drown the voice of a king, he can roll them to drown the questions of a fool!"

"Ah, but he rolled them at the order of Robespierre!" This smoothly barbed shaft drove home most cruelly. Danton could not forgive Robespierre for having cheated him of killing Louis Capet. "And perhaps you will hear them rolled to drown your own voice, Citizen Danton—again at the order of Robespierre."

Accurate prophecy was not difficult in these days.

"And you—you!" Danton emitted a bellow of anger. "You in your fine cravat and fine clothes,

A WATCHDOG BETRAYS HIS MASTER

who talk of Brittany to cloak your own designs—"

The livid face of a corpse emerged from the obscurity behind the two, and a quietly decisive voice struck in.

"Who should not talk of Britanny?" it said. "Danton, you do not know; Saint-Just, you do not realize; but I know and realize, since I myself am from the west! On the first of this month, twelve thousand volunteers left Paris to subdue the Vendée. To-day, seven thousand are dead. This day week, not four thousand will remain alive."

The speaker was Fouché, representative of Nantes.

"Bah!" cried Danton. "In the army of Rochelle alone, Biron has eighty thousand men, a third of them veterans from the Rhine!"

"Not enough by half," retorted the cold, precise Fouché. "Look! In Maine, an army under Jean Chouan is in rebellion against the draft laws. Farther on in the Vendée, the entire country is in arms, and Cathelineau is destroying regiments, capturing cannon, firing towns. Brittany is in civil war. In Normandy, our best soldiers are being massacred. The English are trying to obtain a landing point, and Prince de Talmont is endeavoring to bind all these rebellious forces into one great movement. At all costs, we must block these aims! Citizen

19

SAINT MICHAEL'S GOLD

Danton, forget Prussia and look to the west—the ulcer must be destroyed before France can face the external foe!"

The other two were silent. They might well listen to Fouché, already one of the most prominent men in the convention. His insight, his craft, his balanced brain, constituted a deadly and unerring force. Like Paine, he had a rare common sense, but he also had the personal magnetism Paine lacked, and in later days it carried him to a dukedom.

Suddenly Danton caught a glimpse of me, and swung around.

"Ah!" he exclaimed. His bloodshot eyes glared at me like those of a wild beast. "Ah, here is our American friend, our humanitarian, our fine aristocrat who cannot see a woman's neck bared to the knife! Citizen Martin undoubtedly sees events very clearly. Tell us, citizen, whence comes the danger to our France? Come, instruct us in the cause!"

Soft and deadly words these, horribly instinct with menace. Now I knew Danton had abandoned me utterly, beast that he was! I met his gaze and flung caution aside.

"From ambition," I said.

"Oh!" Danton sneered. "Remarkable! We have nobles who are one with the common people, priests and bishops who lead our armies, and Americans— who are prophets! Come, my citizen from across the sea, prophesy!"

"With pleasure," I said coolly. "You seek to rival Robespierre, who killed a king. Very well, Danton the butcher! If you wish, you may bring a queen to the guillotine. But be careful lest you are dragged in the wake of this ambition, and go the same road."

Danton erupted in a howl of incoherent fury, not lessened by the cynical laughter of Saint-Just or the cold chuckle of Fouché. He flung a mad oath at me and then rushed away. Fouché touched me on the shoulder as I was passing and checked me, staring at me from his dark, deep-set, piercing eyes.

"If I were you, citizen, do you know what I should do?" he asked.

"What, then?" I demanded.

"Take wings," said Fouché, with his slow and terrible smile. "Take wings and fly to your America—within the hour!"

I read a well-meant warning in these words and nodded.

"Thank you, Fouché. Perhaps I shall do so."

Going on, threading my way among the groups,

21

SAINT MICHAEL'S GOLD

I gave up all thought of seeking my seat and remaining for the session. By this time, it was clear that I was utterly lost. My appearance, instead of calming my fellow members, only infuriated them, and I had lost my only chances of help. I must get away at once, or never.

For me, it was the end. During all these months I had used my position and abilities to help unfortunate women and children away from Paris. This, indeed, was my sole excuse for remaining. I had come to France, summoned by Lafayette, two years previously. Like Paine, I was fired by hopes of giving my aid to this revolution in the old world; the idea of carrying help from America to France had enthused me mightily.

Now, however, I was older. With Paine and the others my utter folly stood clear, all illusions were gone. France had finished with revolution and was entering into madness. The patriots, indeed, the Girondins and the noblest of those who had led the way to freedom, were already doomed. As Danton truly said, in a revolution the power gravitated to the most wicked and the basest.

I struggled to reach the entrance again. "I'll go, if I can get out of the country," was my despairing thought. "After all, my time has not been wasted

A WATCHDOG BETRAYS HIS MASTER

—I've saved a few poor souls from the teeth of the wolves, and have brought a touch of pity into this ravening city. Laurent Basse is powerful; he, if anyone, can get me out of Paris, probably has arranged it—"

Again my way was blocked by a wild throng. This eddied away and left two men—rather, one man and a frightful caricature of humanity. The man, who was some obscure Breton deputy, was speaking eagerly, warmly, to the caricature.

"Absolutely forgotten, I tell you! And yet it is the greatest treasure in all France. I have seen the list of it—incredible! Citizen Fromond urged me to speak of it to you. No one has remembered it—"

"I have remembered it," said the caricature. Here was a dwarfish figure with its stoop, disheveled and dirty, blotched, branded by disease, mouth sprawling and huge, red eyes hideous. This creature was the idol of the populace, the most powerful man in Paris, who had risen over all enmity and opposition to a place almost supreme. Marat.

"I have already made arrangements concerning it, but the matter must remain secret," he went on. "Above all, Danton must not sniff it. He has a nose for treasure, that Danton."

23

"Yet," objected the deputy, "how can it be secretly managed? If the Whites seize the place, and they are already working north, they will get it. Such a treasure—"

"It will be managed," said Marat. Looking past the Breton, he saw me, and a mirthless smile twisted his lips. "The trouble in the west amounts to little. Leave all to me."

"Citizen, the trouble amounts to revolution!"

"Be quiet."

Marat pushed him aside impatiently and turned to face me. His blotched and livid visage broke into a snarl, and wild hatred flamed in his eyes.

"So, Citizen American, you have repaid hospitality with insult, and our welcome with treachery!"

I lifted my brows. "Eh? Your meaning, Marat?"

"I know everything!" he burst out with sudden heat. "I know how, at seven o'clock yesterday morning, you escorted a coach past the barrier of the Champs Elysées and on through the guards. In this coach were the ci-devant Baronne de Florelle and her two daughters—eh? You have been indiscreet, citizen."

"I have been merciful," I said, meeting his hot gaze.

A WATCHDOG BETRAYS HIS MASTER

"That word has been forgotten, except by Louisette."

Thus Marat always referred to the guillotine.

"The convention," I said, "has not passed a decree against mercy."

"The decree was passed when the head of Louis Capet fell. And, my American, no decrees are necessary against traitors!"

"Then look to yourself!" I exclaimed angrily, swept by loathing of the creature. "All around you are traitors! Your most intimate friend is the ci-devant Marquis de Montaut. Citizen Cloots, who proclaims God as his personal enemy, was a baron. Citizen Charles Hesse was a prince. Saint-Just was a noble—"

"Enough," intervened Marat with ominous calm, transfixing me with his bestial eyes. "Three days ago, Citizen Martin, I was considering giving you an army to lead. To-day, however, I promise you a wife."

"You are kind," I said. "Her name?"

"Louisette."

With this one word Marat smiled and then was gone in the vociferous throng.

I made my way out of the accursed place, knowing I had heard the very voice of death at my ear.

SAINT MICHAEL'S GOLD

Yet the irony of it brought a laugh to my lips—
Marat the all-powerful about to destroy me, while
his servant was rescuing me! Yet, could Laurent
Basse manage it? This remained to be seen. I
must leave Paris at once, and then France; and
here was a difficult matter. Anyone could enter
Paris, but leaving the city was a problem.

It was drawing toward the hour of my appointment with Basse, so I turned at once toward the
Pont Neuf, the rendezvous being at a café on the
other bank. Once I saw Basse, I could join Rabaut
and get off—if nothing happened to stop me. At
any moment I might be arrested. My figure was
fairly well known and was too large for disguise,
and spies were everywhere.

I saw many persons whom I knew, but who did
not speak to me—nobles and priests in ragged garb,
a wigged nun selling fruit, a marquis pushing a
barrow of clothes for sale. Men were drilling,
children were dancing, people were eating in the
streets and playing cards in the gutters, throngs
were excitedly discussing events or listening to
orators. The people now owned Paris—it was
theirs. The walls were gaudy with placards. In
the Tuileries gardens grew grain in place of
flowers. Beneath all this was starvation, mob law,

26

somber desperation, just as France herself was mad turmoil and confusion with the enemy at her throat.

Fortunately, I had some gold in my belt. The assignats of the republic were practically worthless, and Paris was flooded with false English-made assignats—a shrewd blow at the credit of the republic. Only gold was of avail in a pinch, and I was certainly in a pinch.

"Once I get back to Virginia, I'll stay there," was my morose thought. "That is, if I get back! How the devil Marat discovered my activities—ah! This seems to be a day of meetings."

I had come to the Pont Neuf and started across the bridge when, coming toward me, pushing her wheeled cart of trinkets, ribbons and lavender-water, I perceived Mother Pitou.

A bent and gnarled Parisian hag was she, brown-faced, toothless, crooked in body. Few people dreamed how faithfully she served many of her old masters, how many of the former aristocracy she had aided to leave the city. Also, she served as a royalist agent and spy, and was undoubtedly connected with half the plots and counter-plots going on. Paris was filled with spies, naturally, yet this old hag was an actual worker. She did things.

She nodded to me, and since no one was close at hand, I halted and spoke.

"Good day, Mother Pitou! Is all well with you?"

"I hope so," she said, with a sharp look. "What about the three sparrows?"

"All safe through and on their way under escort," I told her. "It gave me plenty of work getting them disguised and through the barriers, I can tell you! But I had to use my name, and now the game's up. Marat knows."

"Oh!" She was taken aback, then cackled in laughter. Little she cared. "He knows, eh? Then you can slip away, and take with you a little starling who needs your help. He left Paris but was stopped at Versailles—is held there. If you can vouch for him, he'll be set free—"

"Not I," was my angry response. This was not the first time the old beldame had tried to involve me in her endless intrigues. "I'll have nothing to do with your plots, as you well know. When it's a question of helping women away, I'm at your service—or have been."

"But listen, you talker!" She reached out a skinny claw and clutched me by the arm. "Kerguelec is the name—a Breton lad. In reality, one of the de Rohans—ha! The name touches you, eh?"

A WATCHDOG BETRAYS HIS MASTER

"Not a bit." I shook her off, none too gently, for she was a persistent old creature. "Let your aristocracy go to the knife, for all of me—they deserve it, most of them! And even my helping women is ended now, Mother Pitou. I'm denounced and will be arrested—so I'm off to-day, if I can get clear."

"Devil take you!" she snapped at me. "This Kerguelec is at the inn of the Liberty Cap, and one word from you will save his neck. Since you are going, think of your own neck and do a good action at the last, in the name of the saints! Will that hurt you?"

Her appeal reached me with its reason, and shook my decision. Given a certain degree of honor by the new republic and admitted to a guest-seat in the convention, I had flatly refused to take part in any plottings or to connive at the evasion of royalists. In sober fact, I had scant sympathy with the aristocrats and none whatever with their cause. Regarding women and children, it was a far different matter. There, in lending what aid I could, I could see none of the treachery with which Marat had reproached me, but only mercy and plain decency.

Well, it was all over and ended now! The de

29

Rohans were a princely Breton family, and this caught bird was undoubtedly connected with plots and risings. Now, however, John Martin was no more a guest of France—he was a fugitive trying to save his head at any cost! If, as his final action, he might also save the head of another man, why should he not do it?

"Very well," I said to the old crone. "Your argument is sound enough, and if possible I'll do something for this Kerguelec. I'll probably leave the city by way of Versailles—yes, it might be managed! Still," I added, "I'll not be riding out alone. I expect to be in company with a certain friend of yours—a very dear friend, I believe."

"Eh?" She peered up at me. "Who, then?"

"A certain marquis, a gentleman you delight to honor."

"Who, then?" she snapped irritably.

"The Marquis de Saint-Servaut, at present known as Citizen Rabaut."

She broke into a blether of cursing, and with a laugh I swung off along the bridge. I dared tell her nothing of my plans, naturally, for a breath might ruin Laurent Basse.

Gaining the left bank, I walked on to that narrow, gray little street called Ci-git-le-cœur, "Here rests the heart," where in more ancient days the patron of Cellini had builded a house for one of his many loves—perhaps any one of these tall blank structures overhanging the narrow way had named the place. House and love and king all alike forgotten, the words lingered plaintively from the dead past, an echo of what had been and would not be again.

Only a short distance from the quay was the café of the Bonnet Rouge, and pushing open the door, I entered. It was just three o'clock. Over the heads of a few drinkers, I beheld the sprawling figure of Laurent Basse, on the settle at the far end of the tavern. Basse was not an inviting personage. Like his master, he was extremely dirty and unkempt, besides being ferociously hairy; but at present he was to my eyes an angel of mercy.

"How goes it?" he said with a grin, as he gripped hands with me and made room. "You're a lucky devil to have a man like me for friend!"

"Conceded," I replied, as I settled down beside him and watched him shred tobacco into a pipe. "And how goes it with you?"

"Excellently. All the world is being denounced, or soon will be. Louisette will have a deep drink in another day or so!" Basse exultantly pounded on the table with his knife-haft. "Confusion to all aristocrats! If you were an aristocrat, I'd not help you, even though I owe you my life! But you're not. You're an American, and I have a feeling for Americans, me. They laugh. They do not walk with their noses in the air, like the English. Yes, when you pulled me away from those pikes last year, you did yourself a good turn! I don't forget when a man saves my life."

"Well, I'm no aristocrat," I said, laughing. The fellow was as garrulous as a fishwife. "By the way, I met Citizen Rabaut. He spoke of matters I didn't understand in the least, but I am leaving with him in an hour and a half."

Basse grinned again, and called for wine. He flung a coin on the table—real coin, no paper! The wine was hastily brought, the coin pouched, and we were left alone.

"It is curious, a real jest!" Chuckling, Basse stared at me. "You are lost because Marat knows you help women escape. He thinks you are a spy for the Whites, too, but I know better. Me, I agree with him—I like to see a pretty girl kiss Louisette! It is fine to see the red smocks and the proud looks. However, I do not mind if a few get away, since it pleases you. The curious contrast, my friend, is this: You are saved, because Marat has remembered something."

"Salvation is several hours away yet," I said drily.

"Bah! I have your papers in my pocket—Marat signed them in his bath." Basse clapped me on the knee. "Did you know the doctor has ordered him to take baths? It is true, poor devil; I'm sorry for him. Me, I haven't had a bath in two years, and I'm the picture of health. Here's a great joke for you of the convention! Yesterday one of the Girondins accosted Danton in one of the halls, and threatened him furiously, saying it wasn't Marat or Robespierre they feared, but only Danton, who could sway the crowd with his frantic oratory. Well, Robespierre was standing only four feet away! Ten to one he has Danton's head inside a fortnight."

"Let him have it and welcome," I returned with a shrug. "My only present interest is in my own head."

"True." Basse uttered a laugh. "Well, that is safe enough, and a cleaner head than most, eh?" He nudged me enjoyably. "Why do you have red hair, my friend, and bright blue eyes, and a keen straight mouth like that of Saint-Just? A difficult head to disguise. Well, it is safe—because Marat has remembered something."

"Does he ever forget anything?"

"This is what everyone has forgotten, it seems, except a nosy procureur in Avranches, one Fromond by name who kills priests and destroys churches. *Voilà le diable!* A madman, this Fromond, but one to make the dogs dance on the boulevards, I assure you!"

This was the third time to-day I had heard the name uttered.

"Regard, now—there is a treasure sealed away somewhere in Normandy, a place called the Mont Libre. It had another name in the old days, but I forget it. You see our volunteers of Paris without shoes, half naked, fighting and dying so—and this treasure in the provinces! Marat is going to convert it into shoes before Danton discovers it."

"And Citizen Rabaut is to do the converting."

"Everybody is to do it." Laurent Basse pulled his mustache and grinned. "What devils you Americans are for explanations! Nominally, the job falls to this procureur, Fromond. The committee at Avranches will send along a spy to watch him, in shape of a jeweler to weigh and buy in

34

the treasure. Oh, Marat takes care of everything! I have seen the letters. Rabaut is commissioner in charge, to watch the others, and be directly responsible."

"What trust in the fidelity of our citizens!" I said ironically. Basse shrugged.

"Who is to be trusted, these days? Well, the Whites would like to lay hands on this gold, be sure of it, and the roads are unsafe. So, associated with Rabaut, to watch him and take charge of the party's safety, is Citizen Merlin—you may know the man. A jolly rascal from the Faubourg St. Antoine, who helped Javogues empty the royal tombs in St. Denis."

I nodded. The man was one of the lesser Parisian demagogues, followers of Marat.

"All very well, Basse," I said, "but where is my place, and how could I leave Paris? All the barriers are watched closely, in every section. If an order for my arrest is issued, I dare not show my papers—"

Basse cocked an eye at me and solemnly intoned the republican shibboleth.

"Unity, the republic indivisible, liberty, equality, fraternity, or death! *Vive la nation!* Death to aristocrats! Have a drink."

I laughed with the rascal, and our cups were re-filled. Then I repeated my query.

"All very well—but where do I come in?"

"Where Merlin goes out—honest Merlin does not yet know of his appointment, for I have no intention of telling him."

Laurent Basse chuckled in his whiskers, leaned forward, and lowered his strident voice.

"Listen! Me, I can write. Me, I know how little a thing it is to cross an 'l' and make it into a 't', and deftly change a Merlin to a Martin—there, you comprehend? I was charged to deliver the commission to Citizen Merlin and keep it secret. Instead, I change it a trifle and deliver it to Citizen Martin!

"Chances for slips? Yes, a dozen, but none happened. I had to give Rabaut his orders and letters, so I told him you were commissioned. The thing was arranged last night, Marat signed the papers this morning; Rabaut departs this afternoon. To keep him busy, I put him on the track of some good horses—and there's the whole thing in a nutshell."

Laughing, he leaned back and sipped his wine.

The audacity of the man was startling, yet proved his friendship as nothing else would have done.

36

A WATCHDOG BETRAYS HIS MASTER

He knew, of course, that I was no conspirator and no White, as the royalists were termed—that all I wanted was to get away safely. I had saved his life, he was saving mine.

"Good man," I said. "But won't this get you into trouble?"

He roared with mirth at this question.

"Me? Me, the proof-courier of the 'Friend of the People'? Me, the porter of Citizen Marat, whom they call his watchdog? If there is an inquiry, I made a mistake. Upon my word, Laurent Basse can make mistakes with impunity! But if you once get out of Paris, there'll be no fuss about it. Marat is a busy man."

"Basse, I thank you with all my heart—"

"Bah! Our slate is cleared, then, and here's luck all around." He lifted his glass, touched it to mine, and we drank. Then, wiping his mustache, he leaned forward. "You see what you must do?"

"Explain."

"Let us suppose you are out of Paris. Well, can you get out of France? That's another matter. Use your commission and go with Rabaut on this errand. Nobody here will suspect you of having gone to Brittany, with an idea of escape. Nobody will ever imagine how you vanished, unless Merlin shows his face to Marat some day. Well, you'll get to the west safely!

"The whole west is a madhouse. Our honest Blues are destroyed right and left—those devils of Whites are all in arms, and neither side gives quarter. Down with the aristocrats! Let the Widow Capet and the Little Capet die, and we may have peace. Well, the west will be swept by armies presently, the country exterminated! Like the Basques, down there all of them are priests or nobles. But once there, you'll find shelter and you'll be safe— I've given you the start, friend American, and the rest of the game is in your own hands."

These words did not jibe with Marat's scornful dismissal of the Vendean troubles—yet proved that Marat knew all about them. This bestial demagogue knew everything, and could also dissimulate his knowledge; he was the ablest of the triumvirate. Had he lived only a few weeks longer, I verily believe, there would have been no Terror. It was inaugurated by the others as a measure of self-protection, but with Marat alive there would have been no "others" left.

Laurent Basse produced some papers, pawed them over with his filthy hands, selected one with the heading "Committee of Public Safety," and passed

A WATCHDOG BETRAYS HIS MASTER

it to me. Under the words "Year One of the Republic" was written the date, the new calendar not
yet being adopted, and then:

> "Full powers are granted to Citizen Mar-
> tin under the orders of Citizen Rabaut,
> delegated Commissioner of Public Safety."

To this paper were affixed three signatures—
those of Danton, Marat, and Robespierre.

"Yet this is incredible!" I lifted puzzled eyes
to the hairy face of Basse. "This errand is a secret
matter known to Marat alone, yet the others have
signed—"

Basse laughed heartily.

"Listen! Danton uses the army for his own
purposes, Robespierre uses Louisette for his own
purposes, but my master uses both these others for
his own purposes! Judge which is the greatest
man! The others know nothing of Rabaut's real
errand; ostensibly, he goes as commissioner to the
army. I've given him all the documents. And now
let me tell you something else, my friend."

Basse tapped me on the arm impressively.
"About yourself. To-night you will be arrested.
To-morrow you will be sentenced; the day after,
to the knife! If I were you, I'd remember."

39

"No danger," I responded. Rising, I held out my hand to him. "And thank you—"

"Wait!" He broke into a sudden laughter, clinging to my hand. "I met Legendre on the way here—you know Legendre, the butcher! Well, he has sniffed out a pretty joke, this species of a duck! It seems that an innocent Breton yokel, goatskin shirt and all, has been here in Paris for a week or so—and fastened upon whom, think you? Fayau, of all men! Fayau, who wants to burn the whole Vendée and make it a desert! Fayau thought the rogue was a Blue, took him everywhere, exhibited him—Fayau!"

Laurent Basse fell back on the settle, roaring with mirth uncontrolled. I well knew the wild Fayau, who would have suppressed the western risings with barbarous means. I could guess what was coming, and my lips twitched.

"Legendre sniffed something?"

"Aye, the butcher has a nose! He sniffed this stripling for a de Rohan—a de Rohan, mark you! An émigré, a spy, a plotter! And this is on the head of poor Fayau, who would give his right arm to bring a Rohan under the knife! More than this," and pressing one hand to his aching side, Basse laughed out the climax, "more than this, a

girl! One Marie de Rohan, of the accursed princely family! Think of Fayau—"

"They've caught her?"

"She's escaped. Oh, they'll bring her in, never
fear! Legendre is moving heaven and earth to
find her, and Fayau is a raving maniac. Well, luck
to you, luck to you! At least you're no aristocrat.
You're a good fellow, you are. Adieu!"

"Adieu, and all things," I said, and so left him.

CHAPTER III

OUTSIDE, I followed the quay slowly
downstream, having plenty of time left.
Presently I halted and stared abstract-
edly at the brown muddy current below, still swollen by the spring rains. Although I was a republican, I did not share Paine's atheistic ideas, and a
sense of wonder struck me at the workings of provi-
dence as brought forth this day.

The girl, Marie de Rohan, for example. She
was, of course, the Kerguelec of whom Mother
Pitou had told me. Why the old hag had not mentioned her sex, was a mystery. She was no mere
escaping refugee, but an active agent of the
Whites. She had come to Paris, perhaps bringing
letters, and her bold game had won until the last

42

THERE IS ALWAYS THE FUTURE

moment—yet it was not usual for a French woman to be thus employed. There was something more behind it, I concluded, something compellingly personal, perhaps some relative in one of the prisons.

Now Kerguelec was suspected and detained at Versailles. As yet, apparently, Mother Pitou was the only person in Paris to know of it—in Paris, where all the world was wildly hunting the simple Breton lad! It was a keen jest, and like all good jests, had about it a touch of the ironic, the tragic. Fate might overtake Kerguelec at any moment, might well clutch him down before I reached Versailles to-night. Well, we would see!

For the moment I had other matters to occupy my thoughts. To-night arrested, to-morrow condemned, the next day beheaded! An excellent program to remember, as Basse had advised.

"All right, I'm through here, no longer a guest of France," I thought. "Once more I'm an American and nothing else. Everything I've gained here is swept away, so let it go! From this time on, all this murdering crew can look out for themselves if they get in my way. I'm bound for home, and nothing shall intervene."

It was an uplifting thought, a spurring thought. I had suddenly become a hunted man, and I welcomed the work lying ahead of me. Not for nothing had I traveled Indian trails in Kentucky and crossed the western regions of Ohio—if things came to a scratch, I could abandon Rabaut and strike out alone. Liberty was ended in France, as it everywhere ends when it becomes tyranny.

Nor was I any mere soldier of fortune, to shift sides for hire. Fighting for England made no appeal to me, and I had no desire to join the Whites against the cause of liberty—despite everything this cause still remained, and for me it now remained doubly— I would fight for John Martin and home again!

So resolved I turned from the river and threaded my way among the narrow streets to the Rue Dominique. On the way I bought a riding cloak and pistols, and reached the quarters of Citizen Rabaut promptly at four-thirty in no little apprehension. If Rabaut had discovered anything in the interim, I was lost.

Sighting two saddled horses before the door, however, my relief was immediate. Rabaut appeared a moment later. He was quite unsuspicious, flung me a gay greeting, and in five minutes we mounted and were riding away. We were ostentatious enough, too, with our pistols and flaming tricolor sashes and cockades. Just as our own American democracy's

44

THERE IS ALWAYS THE FUTURE

first action had been to institute an order of chivalry, so the new French democracy played like a child with badges and colors and tinsel.

Our traverse of the city was without incident, save to emphasize the tremendous power of the documents we carried. At the sectional barriers where all had to show their papers, we were passed with salutes and cheers; the name of Rabaut was well known, his new authority was impressive, and nowhere was any demand made upon me—as his companion I was not even suspected. This made me smile to myself. Citizen Rabaut might have to answer a few questions later on, if my escape were traced!

At five-thirty we were past the barriers and heading for Seve and Versailles, free.

And now I knew the astounding bit of trickery had actually succeeded. With luck, anything might succeed in Paris, yet in these days luck was a mighty fickle jade. Only a jest prevented Truchon from rescuing Princesse de Lamballe, and a misunderstood word sent Madame Elizabeth to the knife.

Feeling myself thus saved, I turned my attention to the farther objective. I knew the dangerous character of my companion, and yet was confident in my ability to twist him to my purposes. Rabaut, in common with others, felt a certain reassurance

45

from any contact with me or Fournier or Paine; an American might not be entirely understood, but he was at least no spy or informer, had no ulterior motives.

"Fouché said to-day," I observed, as we rode side by side along the two leagues of winding road, "that affairs in the west are in frightful condition and our cause there wavering."

To my utter surprise, Rabaut smiled in his mirthless, sardonic way.

"Let the wolves destroy each other!" he exclaimed, and snapped his fingers. "What will happen? South of the Loire, all the Vendée is in a flame of revolt; those peasants will cross the Loire, meet an army, and be crushed. In Brittany and Normandy the towns are Blue, the country White; the country will be devastated and crushed. In Maine, Jean Chouan may scatter one or two armies—the third will crush him. Cathelineau is a guerrila, to be hunted down and crushed."

"Our journey in Normandy may not be uneventful, though," I said.

"Bah! We should reach Mont St. Michel safely enough—eh?"

Mont St. Michel—now the Mont Libre! Thus suddenly the object of our quest burst upon me, for

THERE IS ALWAYS THE FUTURE

until now I had not recognized the new name of the place.

It held me silent and thoughtful for a space. I had often enough heard of this dreaded rock, an island just off the Breton coast, a solid mount of masonry equally infamous with the Bastille as a royal prison where men rotted; horrible tales were told of it. Upon the revolution, monks and jailers were turned out, and the dungeons became stuffed with priests—men too old or infirm for deportation. The wholesale murder, now on its eve in Paris, had not yet reached the provinces as a general thing.

"The treasure there is said to be enormous," I observed presently. "Do you think we'll find it intact?"

"Why not?" was Rabaut's cynical answer. "Outside Paris, the revolution is not yet ended. Men who fight for a cause do not fill their pockets. Our chief object will be to reach there before Cathelineau or the English make a raid and take the place."

"More exactly," I amended, "our chief object will lie in getting from town to town in safety. The entire countryside, I understand, bristles with muskets for Blues."

"That will be your affair," he said indifferently.

"Then my affair begins at Versailles."

SAINT MICHAEL'S GOLD

"Eh?" Rabaut turned in the saddle with an inquiring glance. "Explain."

I gestured ahead. "At the inn of the Liberty Cap is a Breton lad named Kerguelec. He is held for investigation. Well, I propose to set him free and take him with us."

"And why, in the fiend's name?" asked Rabaut, staring at me.

I touched my gay sash. "Think you we can ride through Normandy like this? We must take off our colors when leaving town—why draw bullets from every hedge? If a road is closed, we shall have to find other roads. Here is a chance to get a Breton guide, who'll know all the western roads. Bound to us by a tie of gratitude, he should serve us well."

Rabaut nodded, and for a space rode on in thoughtful silence. Glancing at this dark, cruel, determined profile at my side, for a fleeting instant I had the impression of strange thoughts passing behind the mask of a face. And here I was right.

"You know our errand?" asked Rabaut suddenly.

"Yes."

"Hm! Marat trusts you. Well, tell me something! What are you Americans doing here—eh? You, Paine—all of you! What have you to gain?"

At this final word, an astounding explanation of

the man beside me flashed over my mind. So astounding was it, that I hesitated to accept the implication.

"Gain?" I repeated. "What have we to gain? Well, I think we came here with visions. Those visions may still persist with the others, for naturally one wants to see the end of such events. For me, personally—"

I hesitated and broke off. Rabaut turned and gave me a searching look.

"Come, Martin, be frank! All men have something to gain; idealism persists only under oppression. The revolution, as you say, began with visions and ideals. It has crumbled and disintegrated into a fratricidal struggle for power. Now it is only a question of what each man seeks. The revolution is ended."

True enough. In these words I could read darkly ominous hints—less in the words themselves than in their tone and accent. Rabaut was feeling me out, carefully exploring my mind. He knew perfectly well I was no mere spy set to watch him.

"I think," was my slow response, "we understand each other, Rabaut. I don't suppose you want to discuss the past; and there I'm one with you! The future alone is interesting."

49

SAINT MICHAEL'S GOLD

"Right!" He leaped at this bait with a swift access of savagery. "The past be damned! I think we shall reach an understanding, you and I. Now, as to this Breton at Versailles—you believe he'll be useful?"

"Very."

"Who told you of him? What do you know about him?"

"Basse mentioned him," I said. "There's little doubt he is a White—perhaps a spy. What matter? He can serve us."

This cynicism struck him in the right spot.

"Agreed, then. What do you say to picking him up and getting dinner, then going on—eh? Neausle is only eight leagues from Paris. We might press on there to-night."

"Willingly."

I smiled to myself as we rode along, for now slow comprehension was coming to me. Rabaut knew the rapidity with which things happened in Paris, knew that at any moment our mission might be countermanded and ordered back—and he wanted to keep ahead of possibilities.

Clearly enough, I began to see into the heart of this rascally man. Once Rabaut had been a marquis, an aristocrat, a man of high position ruined by gam-

50

ing. Now he was a renegade, hated and feared by all, trusted by those he served, and in a way powerful. Another turn of the wheel could land him anywhere, and in these times the wheel turned swiftly.

We rode a space in silence, now across the river and drawing near Versailles. One world was behind us, another ahead. Behind lay Paris and all its madness, its bloody internal strife, its gathering Terror. Ahead of us lay all France. True, each town had a committee, those terrible committees of public safety soon to become agents of murder, yet the two of us carried documents making us supreme over any other man or group outside Paris itself.

"Here is a tremendous contrast," I said abruptly, pointing to the town ahead. "We ride free, and all before us is at our feet. Here, we are masters to be obeyed, responsible to none, and the motto of the revolution becomes a mockery. When we return—"

I paused, and Rabaut uttered a harsh laugh.

"When? You should say, if! Think you I'll be in a hurry to re-enter Paris and give up my powers? Tell me, my American friend, will you be in a hurry—eh?"

"Not I."

"We shall understand each other," he said again, with a certain grim satisfaction.

SAINT MICHAEL'S GOLD

Had I been French, of course, he would not have spoken thus, but I was an American, and perhaps he had some little suspicion of my late activities. In a sense, sundered though we were by a yawning gulf, we were impelled by very similar feelings. Not mere relief at my own escape filled my whole heart—no, there was more, much more than this! Now I could realize how every moment back there in Paris had been one of high tension, of suspense and expectation, of energetic life at full flood where one never knew what might happen next.

Now all this lay behind and past, like an evil dream, and I wanted to see it no more. A wonderful hour, this ride with its realizations of freedom and self-consciousness! Caught up on the wavecrest of public excitement and held there riotously, the individual had been less than nothing in a forced conformation to liberty's shibboleth. I felt myself robbed of two years of life, while sitting there seeing history made around me and helping to make it. The wildest excesses of the revolution were yet to come, but I could feel them impending, had heard them discussed—everything from a new calendar to a new deity in place of God.

The wild wave was nearly at height, and in a short time it would become a seething maelstrom. I could

THERE IS ALWAYS THE FUTURE

scarcely think in sane terms of life as it had been and would be again, in my own land across the sea. This emergence from Paris was a breath of sanity, of relaxation. The remembrance of this very day in the convention hall brought a shiver—so far away it seemed, so incredible and unreal! What had it to do with the cool night air, and the new stars, and the voices of birds?

Instinctively, I sensed much the same feeling in my companion. Here was a strong and subtle man who had betrayed others right and left, handing over his own caste to the knife, a renegade dog become leader of the wolf-pack, holding himself above the tide of events at all costs. He was absolutely sure in himself—there was the keynote to Rabaut. He had respect, fear, reverence, for nothing; having seen his old world destroyed around him, he worked upward in the new with ruthless tread. Yet now, perhaps, Citizen Rabaut wished fervently to get out of it all. He was one of the few men in Paris who knew greater horizons, who could visualize the round earth and not merely little Paris and France. Much blood lay upon the head of Rabaut, and curses, and these worried him not at all—but the future did worry him. With cause.

"At which inn—the Liberty Cap?" he queried, as

53

we rode into Versailles. "Good. The local committee have their headquarters there. We shall dine well—eh?"

Twilight was gathering fast as we clattered along the streets. Before us showed an inn loudly adorned with flags, a soldier on guard outside. Other soldiers came running, flung a rope across the street for barrier, shouted orders to halt. Rabaut drew rein.

"We halt, citizens!" he cried. "We seek the committee and dinner. Where are they?"

"Inside together, citizens!" said a sergeant. "You are from Paris? Whither bound?"

"Ah, that's for the committee, citizen sergeant! Bait our horses and lead us."

Dismounting, we entered the inn, while the sergeant stamped ahead of us. In the main room we came upon a vociferous group seated about a big table—the local committee of public safety. It was the same story here as at Paris; dispute, argument, threats hurled back and forth. Candles were glimmering and someone was bawling over a list of suspects who should be seized. Then a silence fell as we came forward, and Rabaut, giving his name, displayed his credentials.

"Read, citizens."

THERE IS ALWAYS THE FUTURE

The commission was handed about. In its wake went whispers and low voices, while eyes stared furtively at us. Versailles was close to Paris, and these men knew well enough the name of Citizen Rabaut. They were suddenly afraid for their heads, hesitated to ask our business, could only gaze and mutter in suspense. A master had appeared among them, and they cringed.

"Come!" Rabaut uttered a cheerful laugh, as he repocketed his document. "Why such silence, in the devil's name?"

"There is no longer a devil," said a gloomy voice. "Devil and God and superstition have all gone together."

"True, citizen, true! But there is a man—a prisoner. I want him." Rabaut glanced at me. "What's his name, Citizen Martin?"

"Kerguelec," I responded. Instant relief fell upon the gathering.

"Ah! That one is upstairs. He has refused to talk, so we were awaiting some instructions about him."

"I bring them," said Rabaut. "Rather, I give them. Let a horse be requisitioned for him. Let him be fed. Let him then ride away with us—and that's all! Now, citizens, what about some food and wine?"

SAINT MICHAEL'S GOLD

Personal fears were thus assuaged; in these days, none knew who might be a spy or a bringer of doom. At once the table broke into a babble of boasting, eager accusations, gossip, suspicions, demands for news. Everything hinged on Paris—what had been done in the convention? Who was denounced? Was Marat really ill? Had the queen escaped?

Rabaut and I seated ourselves, wine and food were brought, a man went to take care of the horses and provide one for Kerguelec, and bustle filled the room. It was taken for granted the man upstairs, "that one" as they called him, rode out to his death. Over the whole place hung the dominating and dreaded presence of Citizen Rabaut, and none knew it better than Rabaut himself.

I could see the consciousness of it in his air, the harshly bitter contempt for all those around, the cruel delight in thrusting forth barbed words to compel sudden pallor. Here was a new Rabaut, the arrogant noble showing through the renegade's mask. This local committee might rule Versailles in terror, yet Rabaut could hale them all to prison by virtue of the commission in his pocket, and he delighted savagely in making them swallow their own medicine. Few in France would have **dared**

56

THERE IS ALWAYS THE FUTURE

play with such men as these in Rabaut's cool fashion —few, indeed, possessed his infernal audacity, his subtle sense of exactly the right word and look that would sway men to fear or obedience. Marat had the same gift, true; yet Marat was guided by certain principles—Rabaut by none.

As for the patriots, they were only too anxious to sacrifice the scapegoat and rid themselves of the unwelcome caller. With a scrape of feet on the sanded floor, Kerguelec was led into the room to face us. And instantly I sensed a thrill, a half-comprehended moment of drama. Sparks leaped from brain to brain, and I could feel the sting of them, though what lay behind it all was still hidden from me.

We looked upon a tall, slender youth clad in typical Breton costume; high, wide black hat, goatskin vest or jacket, full and baggy breeches coming just below the knee. Over one arm was a cloak, and pistols showed in the tricolored sash, for the suspect had been held but not imprisoned. Beneath the hat was a thin, aquiline, dark face expressive of quiet resolution; the long hair, worn to the shoulder in Breton fashion and not retained by any ribbon, completed a disguise most excellent for a woman, so that only if one knew the disguise might truth be suspected.

SAINT MICHAEL'S GOLD

The brown eyes were steady and very clear, poised high above excitement. Yet for all their poise, those eyes were not proof against startled recognition. In the candle-glow, I saw them flash, and Rabaut was not the man to miss it.

"So!" he exclaimed, leaning back. "You know me, citizen?"

"Certainly I do," returned Kerguelec coolly. "It was only the other day that Citizen Fayau pointed you out to me."

"You know Fayau, then?"

"I have spent the past week with him in Paris."

A bold bid this in view of what Laurent Basse had told me about search being made so frantically for Fayau's impostor. Rabaut's sardonic smile showed instantly he had heard the story about the trick played upon Fayau. Fortunately, the smile must have warned Kerguelec to watch his words, and not bait the man before him. I was not worried, since I now knew how little Rabaut cared about patriotic or other principles, save that of self-interest.

"Citizens," and Rabaut turned to the committee, "where are the papers concerning this suspect?"

"They are here, Citizen Rabaut." A dossier was handed Rabaut and he pocketed it.

"Now, Breton, your name?"

THERE IS ALWAYS THE FUTURE

"Jean Marie Kerguelec, from Ardeon in Bretagne."

"To whom did you belong, in the old days?"

"To myself, citizen."

"Ah! Of the petty noblesse—eh?" Rabaut considered this with a nod. "And have you yet dined?"

"No, citizen. I have eaten."

Rabaut broke into a laugh at this response.

"Good! A horse awaits you. Here is Citizen Martin, a member of the convention. We ride together."

"Where?" demanded Kerguelec, without emotion.

"Toward Bretagne."

"Very well."

"A cup of wine all around, citizens, and we'll get off!"

Amid the bustle, I saw those dark, steady eyes sweep to me. Again I discerned in them a glimmer of recognition. This Breton knew me then? Perhaps I, too, had been pointed out to him. Americans were conspicuous in the convention.

Presently the three of us were leaving, accompanied outside by most of the committee. The horses were waiting and we mounted at once under

59

the smoky flare of a flambeau, made our farewells and started away from this the final outpost of Paris.

We clattered along in silence, none of us speaking until we were out of the town, with the glare of the capital suffusing the early night sky behind. I was feeling hugely relieved, while to Kerguelec it must have seemed a dream. Then Rabaut, between us, held out something to the Breton—it was the dossier.

"Take this—destroy it if you like—eh? You are the man who tricked Fayau. No matter."

Kerguelec was dumfounded. Presently he spoke, hesitant.

"The charges against me—have they been dismissed?"

Now happened a strange thing. Undoubtedly we all felt different beings, with Paris gone behind us. That red city vanished, the stars overhead, the quiet countryside all around, brought back humanity and cool sanity to our hearts. All reason had deserted Paris; this was why Reason was soon to be enthroned there in place of God. Here Rabaut could afford to be himself, to slough all the patter of the republican demagogue. He flung out a hand to the stars, and laughed.

THERE IS ALWAYS THE FUTURE

"Bah! There are no charges against you. Look at the night—and ask such a question! I have requisitioned you to aid me, no more. It has saved you some discomfort. Therefore you can afford to repay me—eh?"

Kerguelec evaded. "Saved me discomfort? I think it has saved me a head."

Rabaut turned and regarded him, undoubtedly pondering this evasion. The man was like that, catching at wholly unexpected things.

"So? I do not know you, and do not care what you have done. I have other matters in hand than feeding the guillotine. Is it understood?"

"Yes. Do we really go to Bretagne?"

"To Avranches," said Rabaut curtly.

After a little he leaned over toward me and made a gesture, reining in his horse until it fell behind. I reined in beside him, and he spoke under his breath, in English—he was fluent in several tongues.

"Feel him out. We must know whether we can trust him to repay us—rather, to guide us in case of need, and remain with us, eh? I know these Bretons. Get a promise out of him and we have him safe."

I nodded. Rabaut urged his horse on ahead once more, until he was riding well beyond earshot.

SAINT MICHAEL'S GOLD

I drew in beside Kerguelec and caught a slight laugh, almost a feminine laugh.

"I, too, speak English!" he said softly. "You have the promise, my friend. How did you know of me?"

"From Mother Pitou," I said, then caught the import of his words and started. "You know of me, also?"

"Naturally I do," came the dry retort. "For the past three days I've been trying to reach you with letters. Finally I had to destroy them undelivered."

"Letters?" I exclaimed. "What letters?"

"Well, Citizen Martin, I did not read them, but I happen to know their contents. One was a patent of nobility, with title of Comte. Another was a commission as colonel of horse in the allied army. These can be replaced of course. Another prayed you to join me in my present mission—"

"Are you mad, or am I dreaming?" I broke in. "Count? Colonel of horse? Letters—then from whom are these letters?"

"From the princes, who owe you gratitude and would secure your services."

I checked an angry oath, and then uttered it freely in a new access of anger. What fools these Bourbon princes were! Because I had been doing good

THERE IS ALWAYS THE FUTURE

and quiet work for the sake of humanity, they leaped at the conclusion I would serve them politically in their petty intrigues and plots! My anger became dismayed consternation.

Everything lay clear before me now. If the enemy had spies in Paris, Paris also had spies among the enemy. Probably de Neuville or some other royalist agent had carried similar letters or copies, and they had fallen into the hands of Marat's spies. John Martin made a count, an officer—no wonder Marat's fury had leaped at me!

I gave Kerguelec an unadulterated piece of my mind.

"Worse than folly, it's madness!" I concluded. "Fools that they are to do such things! I want none of your titles of nobility, and none of your gratitude. News of this rank folly has reached Marat, and has nearly destroyed me. Your princes—bah! I have nothing to do with them."

"But with the king?"

"I am an American."

"Then," said Kerguelec softly, "with me?"

"That's different. You're a woman in distress."

Kerguelec caught his breath. "You know?"

"Half Paris knows and is hunting for you," I said grimly. "Marat knows, too, what I've been doing, and now I'm fleeing for my life. Fortunately Rabaut does not suspect it, nor does he know who you are."

Kerguelec laughed. "No! That is evident. If he knew my name—ah!"

I missed a hidden significance in his words. "I've persuaded him to give you a lift, on the plea we might have need of you."

"I understand. Now, my mission with you, or rather the mission on which I hoped to have your help—"

"Leave it," I snapped. "I'm through with everything here. I want none of your plots."

Again Kerguelec laughed, softly, clearly, amusedly.

"It would take you near Avranches. It is partly a private mission, and partly—"

"I refuse it," I said coldly, "and I refuse to talk about it. Now, do you want to get out of France with me, or not?"

"After my errand is done. Where are we bound for, exactly?"

"Mont St. Michel."

Kerguelec remained silent for a long moment, and turning to him I found a look of stark amazement on his smooth, steady features.

64

THERE IS ALWAYS THE FUTURE

"Of all places!" he said, and laughed once more. "Of all places! And afterward?"

"I don't know. All the seaports are in the hands of the Blues. To St. Malo, perhaps, once I'm rid of this Rabaut and can get hold of a boat. I have commissary powers myself, as his assistant."

"Then we stay together, if you wish," came the prompt decision. "You can help me, I you. As for the errand, let it rest pro tem. Those letters really harmed you, or their import?"

"Yes. It must have become known. As though I'd accept a barren title, or sell myself to a foreign prince's service—bah! You in Europe don't know Americans."

"Perhaps not," came the thoughtful reply. "Well, what about Rabaut? You know who he is. You know what he can expect if he falls into White hands. Perhaps you'll be rid of him easily enough. Do you know how I recognized him?"

"No."

"In other days I have danced with him. He denounced my two brothers. They are in prison or dead. That is one reason I came to Paris—to try and get some trace of them. You see now?"

In those words was a certain steely note, indicating the quality of this woman-man. I perceived, indeed, something of what lay behind her presence. I was little astonished by it, and indeed my mind went more to her words regarding Rabaut. His fine head depended wholly upon the brain inside it. If caught by the Whites, this man would be lucky to get off with the fate of Judas—he was not likely to be caught, however. Rabaut was not the man ever to be caught.

"Why did you try to help me, if you would have none of my offered mission?" asked Kerguelec in a low voice. "If you are fleeing for your life, why would you disdain the reward and gratitude of the princes?"

"One answer to both queries, and the same I have already given," I said. "Because I am an American."

Kerguelec pondered this, and we had no more speech together on the matter, for after a little Rabaut slowed down and rejoined us.

The personal equation now perplexed and puzzled me—the presence of the Breton. This girl, a de Rohan, of a princely family in Brittany and one of the noblest in France, had suffered most bitterly at the hands of the arch-betrayer; yet, to save herself, she must now give him her help. It held an odd bite of irony.

THERE IS ALWAYS THE FUTURE

On the other hand, Kerguelec obviously stood in acute peril. Rabaut was fooled for the moment, but if he had known Marie de Rohan in the old days, he would not be fooled for ever. Further, recognition might come in any town, and it would mean death; the blood of a de Rohan would be a sweet savor in the nostrils of all France. I knew, also, how special agents were being sent out into the departments to seek hidden émigrés, Fouché being one of them, and here was another source of peril to the Breton.

As to the proffered rewards, and the hinted mission, I dismissed them all with scarce a thought. I wanted no share in any plot, much less missions for the Bourbons, whom I heartily despised. True, I would have worked for the poor queen, since it was due to her pleading that Rochambeau and Lafayette had gone to help Washington, but she was lost beyond helping. Free of Paris, I was free of everything, and firmly intended to remain free, until I could rid myself of Rabaut and France together. Concerning this ridding, I had dark forebodings. I rather doubted, from the man's hints, whether he had any intention of returning to Paris at all.

So we rode on, each occupied with private thoughts. Once through St. Cyr, we pushed along the three leagues farther to Neausle, a little town lying dark and silent under the stars, for the hour was late.

"To-morrow night we'll make Bressole, and Alençon the next," said Rabaut, as we came into the quiet village street. "That is, with luck aiding us. It'll mean hard riding and no delays—eh?"

"The farther the better," said I, voicing the one thought in all our minds.

Reaching the village tavern, Rabaut lost no time in raising a clamor and announcing himself. At once the title of commissioner set the place in motion. Lights twinkled up, doors were unbarred, a host appeared in his nightgear, and a sleepy half-clad boy led away the horses to the stables.

"Two rooms, a call at sunrise, and breakfast— no mere morning drink," said Rabaut to the host, and turned to me. "You'll share my chamber?"

"Gladly."

Kerguelec left us, having a room to himself. Once we were alone with the door closed Rabaut came to me.

"Well?"

"All settled. He stays with us and will prove a valuable help. He's a White, but we can depend on him."

THERE IS ALWAYS THE FUTURE

"Excellent. And his real name?"

"I didn't ask."

"Hm!" Rabaut scratched his chin thoughtfully, a shadowy frown in his eyes. "Something familiar about that smooth dark face of his—well, let it go, so long as he serves us well! If he cheats the guillotine, I shan't hold it against him. Me, I have other fish to fry, eh?"

I smiled to myself. Somebody was fast betraying a lack of zeal for the republic, and I suspected now what the lure might be.

CHAPTER IV

ON ONE SIDE A LAWYER, ON THE OTHER
A HEADSMAN

HARD riding turned the trick for us, and without incident, other than a meeting with a courier from the west. He had no lack of bad news for Paris—Cathelineau was destroying like an avenging angel, and his peasant army would soon be winning battles. It was a bloody war, with no quarter given on either side. Prisoners, if taken, were shot.

Late at night we came riding into Alençon, horses and riders alike half dead with weariness. Avoiding the old walled city, we made direct for the faubourg of Montsor, on the other bank of the Sante. Here we came to rest at a large inn near the former Benedictine priory. Late as was the hour, we found the host and his people still up and about. It seemed that another traveller had come in shortly before, bound for Paris.

A LAWYER AND A HEADSMAN

"And who may this other rider be?" demanded Rabaut peremptorily, as we followed the host up to our rooms.

"A great man in the west, citizen commissaire! One Citizen Fromond, who comes from Avranches—"

Rabaut halted. "Name of a name!" he cried out, astonished. Then he reached forward and halted the host with a shoulder-grip. "Regard! I must see this man in the morning, citizen—look to it! Let him not depart, or you'll suffer!"

The host promised fervently, and we staggered on to bed. Rabaut was too weary to rouse up Fromond to-night, and I was too dog-tired also to ask questions or pay any attention. The name of Fromond struck sharp echoes in my brain, but a bed was more important than echoes and I was asleep in ten minutes.

The window of our chamber being open, I was wakened in the early morning despite weariness by the banging of carts in the street, as it was a market-day. Rabaut was still snoring away. Without rousing him, I shaved and dressed, went downstairs and obtained a bite to eat. There was no hurry, for we had arranged to stop over the day at Alençon, to rest ourselves and the horses. Rabaut now

71

felt himself beyond any possible recall, and I had quite shaken off all feeling of danger from the rear.

While breakfasting, I took note of a huge fellow sitting in a dark corner, also breaking his fast. His size drew my attention, for it was unusual in a Frenchman; he was even taller than I, much more heavily built, and had a merry countenance. He seemed a droll fellow, for the host was chuckling heartily at his remarks.

The meal finished, I set out for a morning stroll; the day was beginning perfectly, even with promise of heat. Lazily drinking in the warm sunlit air, I sauntered along the wall of the priory, and at a corner was drawn by a commotion. A dozen people stood there about two men, and a harsh, dry voice was crackling high. The expectant, yet hesitant air of those around was enough to show me the cause—here was another such scene of denunciation as had become altogether too common. Some unhappy returned émigré or devoted priest, disguised and still ministering to his flock, was being unmasked and made prey to the red knife.

Coming upon the two central figures, however, I instantly perceived this was no common affair. One man, poorly dressed, white of face, shrank back against a wall, while above him quivered a furious black-clad figure at which I stared hard.

Even in these days of topsy-turvydom and outlandish apparitions, this man immediately arrested the attention and curiosity. Amid fanaticism run rabid, his fanatic air stood out with singular and terrible force. Bareheaded in the morning sunlight, he was denouncing the poor shrinking creature before him—and what denunciation it was! Seldom, even in the wild scenes of the convention, have I heard such vitriolic words.

"Dog of a priest!" he was crying, his voice metallic and piercing. "Ah, I know you! I saw you once in Avranches. Unspeakable dog that you are—"

The remainder was unquotable, fervid with black hatred, so outrageous as to bring up the poor victim into a semblance of dignity. The ragged, dirty, pallid little man straightened himself and met those flaming eyes.

"It is quite true," he said with simple stateliness. "I have not taken the oath prescribed. And I know you, my poor son—my poor Jacques Fromond! I forgive your words and deeds, and shall pray for you."

SAINT MICHAEL'S GOLD

Fromond! The name whipped me swiftly. Not so swiftly, however, as the pity of the priest whipped the black-clad man. He flung up an arm to strike, when I stepped forward and touched him on the shoulder. He swung around and looked at me, teeth bared.

"Away!" he cried. "Away, citizen! This is my prey."

"No," I said calmly, noting how one and another of those standing around exchanged low speech at sight of me. "No, citizen procureur of Avranches, Citizen Fromond! This poor man is not your prey. On the contrary, it is you who are my prey."

Simple words, yet with remarkable effect. These other folk had heard of a commissioner having arrived from Paris, and took me for him. They melted away quickly. I made a significant gesture to the little priest, who scuttled off at once, quite forgotten by his denouncer. Fromond and I were left alone there, he staring at me, breathing rapidly, his whole manner menacing and frightful.

It is hard to describe the man, since he was above mere words. He was fair of complexion, and the left side of his head bore a large bare-shredded patch as from some old wound or injury. In pro-

74

A LAWYER AND A HEADSMAN

file he was remarkably handsome; in full face, he was an unbalanced devil.

One brow and eye were twitched up—the left side again—and the same corner of the mouth drawn down, as though the wound on his head had affected the facial nerve. What a mouth it was! Thin and powerful, bitter, cruel and cold as steel. The eyes were no less horrible to see. Light blue, all ablaze with frenzied energy, they were at once the most furious and the most mournful eyes I have ever seen in a human face—more deeply sad, indeed, even than those of Saint-Just. Mad? Not at all. This man was awfully and terribly sane, I realized, so sane as to be fully conscious of the devil within him.

"Who are you?" he said slowly, aware how the little crowd had melted away. "Who are you, who know me?"

"A messenger," I said. "At the inn is Citizen Rabaut, commissioner sent by the Paris committee. He desires speech with you at once."

This shook him. Obviously the inn-keeper had not yet told him of our arrival, for his jaw fell and his eyes widened on me.

"A commissioner?" he said. "But I have business in Paris, with the committee—"

75

"And the citizen commissioner has business here with you."

Ominous again, and now he caught the full implication. He took a step backward.

"There is some mistake," he said, more quietly. "I am the syndic procureur of Avranches, member of the committee there." A sudden excitement broke loose and leaped within him. "Do you know that I have destroyed the old cathedral and palace? Do you know I have hanged four priests and twelve monks, and shot eight others? Do you know I have stripped bare every church within five leagues—"

"I know only that Citizen Rabaut has business of importance with you," I said coldly. "Must I have you arrested, or will you come and speak with him?"

"Certainly, certainly," he replied, his excitement going as rapidly as it came.

And there I had a clue to him. His fanaticism must be directed wholly against religion, but held no madness; it was a clear, cold, sane fury of bitter hatred. Only paradoxical words can sometimes describe the tremendous paradoxes of human nature. That Fromond's brain was unimpaired, became evident in his prompt reception of fear at my words, his swift abandonment of the victim. Perhaps his rage against all things religious was after all partly assumed—a step to rise upon, a focal cause, just as Robespierre rose by the guillotine, and the Girondins by the betrayal of their king. Yes, reason was active enough in this man's brain! What others took for madness was a self-induced fury, an abnormal rage and zeal for destruction.

"You are a commissioner also, citizen?" he asked, as we turned back toward the inn.

"I am assistant to Citizen Rabaut."

"You speak like an Englishman."

"I am an American."

"Ah!" He halted, turned to me, and with another uprush of eagerness would have embraced me had I not avoided him. "An American! Citizen, I honor you. I honor any citizen of that noble land which has abjured all religion!"

"There you lie," I said bluntly. "The United States has done no such thing."

"But it is set forth in your treaties!" he cried, staring at me. "A friend wrote me about it—statements that your government was in no sense founded on the Christian faith—"

"Oh, the devil fly away with you!" I snapped

roughly at him. "Shut your cursed mouth and come along."

This silenced and angered him, for which I cared nothing.

Something in me crawled at proximity to the man; he gave me the sense of a dangerous reptile. Also, I was myself angry and not at all disposed to bandy words with him. He was symptomatic of half France, revolting against any and all religious faith in a vague brainless fashion. We in America have small patience with any fanatic who strives to bend all the world for or against something, to suit his own petty notions. Our very freedom had been born in revolt against just such efforts, and if ever this hard-won independence of thought and speech were to fail, our very republic would go to crash.

Upon reaching the inn, I learned that Rabaut was not yet up and about. Citizen Fromond, somewhat disgruntled, went in to his breakfast, and I stopped to smoke a pipe on the long bench outside the door. Midway of my smoke, a shadow fell upon me and I looked at the big man I had previously seen in the main room. He was, I judged, a good six foot two, and built in all proportion.

"Good morning, citizen!" he exclaimed, with

A LAWYER AND A HEADSMAN

a nod, and sat down beside me. The bench groaned under his weight. "A fine day and a poor pipe you have there. I know all about pipes. I learned about them from a sergeant in a Rhineland regiment. You shouldn't have to pull at it—badly stuffed, perhaps. Look here! Did you ever hear the story about the clay pipe and the vivandière——"

He chuckled and related a scandalous army tale, with so merry a voice and air that he drew a laugh from me before I knew it. Then, abruptly, he faced me with a sharp question.

"I hear you're the assistant commissioner from Paris?"

I nodded to this. He leaned over, clapped my knee, and winked.

"Listen! Is it true that they're sending a guillotine to the west?"

"I don't know," I said. "I believe some are being sent to the provinces, though."

"Damnation take the thing!" he exclaimed. "I hope the man who invented the accursed contraption will lose his own head by it—serve him right!"

"Dangerous sentiments to express, citizen," I said, surprised by his utter lack of caution. So, at least, his words appeared.

"Nonsense! I've lost my job, thanks to the

cursed guillotine, and have reason to damn it! Look you, friend—since you are commissioners, you'll have need of me! I'll ride with you for my keep and ten francs a head."

I had to laugh at his manner. "Apply to Citizen Rabaut. What's your profession, then?"

"Ask them in Caen the profession of Citizen Tronchet! Presently I'll show you my profession —it shows better than it sounds. I have a fine big Norman horse to carry me, I love a good bottle, a good lass, and a good story, and between ourselves I had as soon kill Blues as Whites at your bidding—always at your bidding, citizen commissaire! I have a liking for your face—you're a man, if I know one. What say you?"

Looking at Tronchet more keenly, I discerned new angles to him. He was jolly enough, his every word provocative of a laugh, yet underneath this I divined things very stolid and firm—more than mere Norman phlegm. Indeed, the man was like a stone wall, yet his surface jollity acted as mask to a penetrating and active brain. Suddenly he clapped me on the knee again and came to his feet, lightly as a feather.

"Here, I'll get my profession and show you!"

A LAWYER AND A HEADSMAN

He vanished inside the inn, laughing to himself, and leaving me to wonder what he had meant by his profession and ten francs a head. However, at this moment I caught the voice of Rabaut shouting for me, and went inside to see Rabaut and Fromond together on the stairs.

"Come along, Martin!" said Rabaut, and started up above. I followed them. The three of us came to our room, and here Rabaut introduced me to Fromond. The procureur gave me a venomous look but said nothing. We sat down, and Rabaut got out his documents.

"Well met, Citizen Fromond—I have letters and orders for you from the committee. More correctly, from Marat."

Fromond sneered coldly. "So my letters and appeals have wakened him after all, then!" He took the papers handed him, broke the seals, and glanced them over with swiftly flaming eyes. "Aye! The treasure of that accursed Mont St. Michel— now Mont Libre! It was on this errand I was riding to Paris. We are well met, indeed. There'll be such a spoiling as the west has never known! Everything is there, safely locked away. The keys and inventory are in Avranches."

"Where?" demanded Rabaut quickly—almost too

81

quickly. Fromond looked at him, and I sensed a clash between the two.

"In my keeping," returned Fromond curtly. "Ha! The cause of liberty shall be well served by the hoards of those accursed monks! Some of the finest gold-work in France is in that place. I have seen it."

"Then it is settled that you ride with us in the morning?" said Rabaut. "We rest here for the day."

"Agreed. I shall be glad to join you. To-day I'll ferret out some of the hidden blackbirds here—"

"You," I intervened, "will do nothing of the sort, Citizen Fromond."

At this blunt speech, Fromond swung toward me with a threatened outbreak of fury, and Rabaut made a gesture of caution, which I disregarded. I knew my man now.

"We are on important business," I pursued coldly, giving Fromond look for look. "Being responsible for the safety of this party, I say you shall do no ferreting, as you call it. Kindly remember it is we who give orders, not you! Our errand lies at the Mont, not here; with gold, and not with fugitive priests. If you stir up some poor

devils, we may be detained heaven knows how
long, or get into endless difficulties."

Rabaut was instantly caught by this intimation.

"Right!" he said with decision. "Citizen Martin
is right. We have an errand to do, and must do
it. You understand, Fromond?"

"Yes," snapped the lawyer angrily. Just then
came a thunderous, imperative summons at the
door of the room. Rabaut lifted his voice.

"Stop that noise and wait until I call! Now,
Citizen Fromond, I have orders regarding a certain
jeweler of Avranches, who is to go with us—"

"I know, I know," put in Fromond with a nod.
"It is Citizen Plessis; we have gone into the affair with him before our committee. He is to accompany us, weigh all the metal, and will buy it
in."

"Exactly. Then we go on to Avranches, pick
him up, get an escort under command of Citizen
Martin, here, and proceed to the Mont. Is all clear?"

"Quite. You have no escort now, then? But
it is scarcely safe."

"We have a Breton riding with us," said Rabaut.
"He is an excellent guide, and we're safe enough
with him. Outside, there! You may enter."

The door was flung open at his call. There stood

my huge Tronchet, grinning merrily at us and leaning on a great two-handed sword, nearly shoulder high to him. He came forward into the room and slammed the door.

"Greeting, citizens! *Voilà,* my profession!"

We all stared at him. Seeing that the man was looking at me, Rabaut gave me an inquiring glance. I laughed.

"Devil take me if I know what it means! This is Citizen Tronchet, who seeks some sort of employment with us. He is out of work, I believe."

Tronchet uttered a bellowing laugh, and this in itself half banished Rabaut's cold frown. He put both hands on the pommel of his sword and chuckled at us.

"Aye, the guillotine has put me out of work, and the republic therefore owes me a living. Besides, think how well you can use me! I know more merry tales than you have ever dreamed, I can kill a horse with one blow of the fist, I can drink a quart of old Calvados and never miss the nick o' the neck, and I am a surgeon who guarantees to cure all human ills at a touch. Consider all this! It will cost you only my keep and ten francs a head, for I provide my own horse, one fit to carry me!"

84

A LAWYER AND A HEADSMAN

Rabaut was fascinated and interested. I began to perceive a sinister something beneath this great joking mountain of a man.

"Name of the fiend!" Rabaut settled back into his chair good-humoredly and almost smiled. "What is your profession, eh?"

"Why, I'm the hereditary headsman of Caen, citizen!"

I started slightly, with sheer astonishment. Fromond took a pinch of snuff nervously. Rabaut opened his mouth, then with a burst of laughter slapped his hand down on the table.

"Good! Good! Citizen Tronchet, you are engaged! Regard Citizen Martin, at my left hand, and at my right, Citizen Fromond. With us also rides Citizen Kerguelec, not present. Now, let us suppose I ordered you to perform the business of your office on, say, our good Citizen Fromond here —eh?"

Fromond's thin features became white. Tronchet tapped the hilt of his big sword; his manner became curt, decisive, cold.

"Then, citizen, you would have to employ a gravedigger."

"So! What if Citizen Fromond ordered you to behead me?"

SAINT MICHAEL'S GOLD

"For that, he must display authority superior to yours."

"Perfect! I see you understand things," and Rabaut chuckled. Glancing at Fromond, however, I saw he did not relish this saturnine jesting, and the look he flung at Rabaut was bitter. "You ride with us, Tronchet. You'll obey my orders or those of Citizen Martin, who is my assistant and is responsible for the safety of the party. Is it understood?"

"Understood, citizen," said Tronchet with a salute. Rabaut gestured to the door, and the headsman departed. Fromond rose and likewise departed, under plea of writing letters. The door closed. Rabaut surveyed me with a satiric smile and drew out his snuff-box.

"Congratulations! We have a good man in this Tronchet. His sword, however, appears oddly rusted—hm! Headsman of Caen, eh? Yes, he's a Norman by looks and speech, as one can see. Well, you heard Fromond? You've chosen to make him an enemy—you'd best beware!"

"So had you," I retorted. Rabaut snarled.

"Aye? Let him dare make trouble, and I'll fling him into jail! He's too sharp for that, though—so I say, beware of him! That man is dangerous."

86

A LAWYER AND A HEADSMAN

I met his perilous eyes and smiled.

"Dangerous to us personally, or to our errand?"

Rabaut frowned. "Did you note his words about the jeweler, who is a spy of the Avranches committee? Look at the thing—all cursed thievery! Fromond hates priests insanely, and wants to rob them, destroy their treasure, see it melted down! The jeweler will buy the precious metals, but at a half of their value, be sure! Sheer robbery all around."

"Then of us all," I said coolly, "perhaps Citizen Fromond is the only one actuated by motives of real disinterest."

Rabaut tapped his snuffbox and stared hard at me.

"Ah!" he said. "And what is your interest in the affair, Martin?"

"The same as yours—if we understand each other."

His face warmed, and he nodded, "Very well," he assented. "After we have bagged the wolf, we shall talk about the skin—eh? It's agreed."

And at this, I knew where Citizen Rabaut stood.

We were a curious company, met this noon about a large table. Two of the local committee had come to pay their respects to the Parisians—filthy knaves, boasting of their past atrocities and those to come. They were full of a new story from some town to the north, about three nobles named de Chaponay, a father and two brothers; these, some days since escaped from prison, were being hunted everywhere. Tronchet immediately applied for the job of beheading them if caught along our route, and Rabaut granted the request.

Fromond already hated me and distrusted Rabaut, yet to some extent he feared us both. Oddly enough, he took an instant liking to Kerguelec, perhaps because the latter could speak Breton, and he had studied the language ardently; they shortly became inseparable. Tronchet, of course, was the friend of everyone from the start. To imagine his real business, unless one could probe below the surface, was impossible.

At this meal, it so chanced, occurred an incident apparently slight, yet one in reality fated to set the seal upon my relations with Citizen Fromond. I sat at one end of the board, Kerguelec and Fromond on my right, Tronchet on my left. The meal was nearly finished, when I caught a dull rattling sound as something fell to the sanded floor; at the same instant, a pallor swept across the face of Kerguelec.

A LAWYER AND A HEADSMAN

I glanced down at the floor, leaned over, and picked up a small rosary with beads and cross of wood. A Breton naturally was inseparable from a rosary, even in peril.

I straightened up and slipped the thing into my pocket, then caught Fromond's gaze and knew he had perceived it. He said nothing, but his light blue eyes were blazing with venom and wild surmise. I met his look with a smile, but he refused the challenge, so I laughed and went on talking to Tronchet.

Afterward, seeing Kerguelec saunter out alone, I joined him and we walked down the street together. At the first opportunity, I slipped the rosary into his hand, with a dry comment.

"After this, if you must carry it, pocket it more securely."

"Thank you," he said quietly. "You should have let me recover it, however. Now Fromond will destroy you if he can. He said to me you looked like a priest in disguise."

At this I broke into laughter uncontrollable—John Martin a priest! Kerguelec flashed me an angry glance.

"You are amused? Look out! I tell you, that man is insane!"

SAINT MICHAEL'S GOLD

"No—he's to be pitied, not feared," I returned. "Don't be too sure of his insanity. Something terrible lies in his eyes, but it's not insanity—more like remorse, to my mind. Ten to one his activity against religion is a sort of mania, pushing him farther all the while, yet at heart bitterly regretted. Because he rebels in his soul against his own actions, he tries to stifle himself and go on to worse— oh, you may laugh at it, but wait and see! Here he comes now. I'll charge him with it to his face."

Fromond indeed was approaching. Kerguelec caught my arm.

"For the love of heaven, abandon this madness! The man is dangerous!"

I shook off the hand. "I'm weary of intrigue and pretense. Now I'll jerk him out into the open for once—ha, citizen! A word, if you please!"

Fromond halted and regarded me fixedly. "What word, priest?" he snapped.

"Just that." I smiled. "Man, you don't fool me for an instant! Give up the pose! How your atheistic fervor started, I can't say, but I know your heart fights against it. You've gone so far you can't draw back now, eh? You're continually trying to prove your own sincerity to yourself, trying to drown yourself in floods of hatred. Well, give it up where I'm concerned. You don't make me believe in you."

My shaft drove home. His face went white as death, and the left side of his countenance twitched. His eyes widened, as though beneath a mortal blow.

"You—you devil!" he gasped. A sudden fury convulsed him; he whipped out a knife and leaped at me, like a maniac.

By good luck I caught one wrist in each hand and stood holding him, for he had little strength and I a good deal—he was like a struggling child. I looked over his shoulder at Kerguelec and winked.

"Go find Tronchet with his sword. Tell him I have work for him."

Kerguelec departed, understanding me. No one else was close by—men watched from some distance only. Those words of mine pricked all Fromond's bubble of mad fury; it was, indeed, a deliberately induced fury. He quieted, looked into my eyes, and let fall the knife. I held to his wrists.

"You mean to kill me?" he asked thickly.

"No, you poor impostor, not unless you force me to it. I'm sorry for you, Fromond! Because a rosary falls to the ground, don't imagine the bearer is a priest. Don't try to make yourself into a devil; you're not a successful devil, Fromond.

91

We're to be companions, and must reach an understanding, if we're to work together. I have need of you, so drop all this pose before me."

He went limp in my hands, trembling as though with an ague. The fury had passed from his eyes, and their sadness was harrowing.

"Need of me?" he repeated dully.

"Wake up! I have not been a priest, but Rabaut has been a marquis. Keep your eye on him, Fromond, especially after we reach Mont St. Michel. Nobody's to be trusted, these days."

The hint startled him, gave him new food for thought. He straightened up and I released his wrists. A light of conjecture flashed into his face.

"Ah!" he murmured.

I left him standing there in the street, staring after me.

CHAPTER V

I WAS deliberate in avoiding any private speech with Kerguelec, after this. Though I knew from his manner how eagerly he desired it, I did not. My own affairs were going on swimmingly, and I had no intention of being drawn into any political intrigues or plots which would complicate things. Kerguelec seemed quite capable of acting his part beyond suspicion. Even knowing the truth as I did, it was nearly impossible for me to discern any hint of the woman beneath the Breton's outer seeming. In this, of course, the costume and long hair helped Kerguelec tremendously.

Taking stock of my own case, I was fatuously unworried. Everything seemed against discovery or pursuit, for at Paris our errand remained a secret mission. Unless Marat caught sight of worthy Citizen Merlin and ferreted out the imposture, he

93

would never dream how my escape had been accomplished. Above all, a man out of Paris was a man forgotten, and Marat was busy scheming, fighting, killing. Or so I thought, like a fool, forgetting how soon the reports must have been turned in that Citizen Martin and Citizen Rabaut had left town together.

As we rode into the west we made an excellent company, and our big Tronchet proved the life of the party with his droll stories and humors. If he were Rabelaisian at times, then Kerguelec laughed with the rest—this was too stern a game for maid's blushes and shrinkings. Yet the huge fellow puzzled me. His tongue slipped on the revolutionary jargon at times, and more than once it seemed he was forcing himself to jollity.

Rabaut drew ever more into himself. Fromond's presence laid check upon him, and the two men rasped each other harshly, almost to enmity. So Fromond for the most part rode with Kerguelec— to my great amusement. Little did the bright-eyed, raving fanatic guess how his friendship lay with one who was not only an aristocrat, but of a family noted for its churchly support!

The roads were strictly watched, all the towns being on the lookout for the three escaped de Cha-

ONE IS NOT ALONE

ponays, father and two sons, but we had no difficulty in pressing forward. So we came to Mortain, a tiny but famous place perched among bleak rocks, riding into the village late one night with the end of our journey looming close. Avranches was only a day's ride away. Our most direct route to Mont St. Michel lay by way of Ducey, but we must pass by Avranches in order to pick up the jeweler and our escort.

Morning brought us disquieting information. The main road to Avranches was most dangerous, the whole countryside being in turbulent disorder. The forests were savage and wild, and in their cover was being waged a war of extermination, chiefly by peasants of both parties. The Parisian soldiers were helpless outside the towns; ignorant of the country, ambushed at every turn, they were only blundering fools, and the veterans were in the same fix. Their case was exactly similar to that of Braddock's grenadiers trying to fight Indians in our own American forests, and these peasants of Normandy had all the guile and cruelty of Shawnees.

Our wakening in Mortain afforded an excellent example of the life hereabouts—it came from a volley of musketry. The half-dozen soldiers quartered on the town had caught a priest, a woman, and three Whites—and this was the result. No quarter was given on either side, none was asked. Family was divided against family. Those who had suffered under the old régime were Blues, those who remained true to king and religion were Whites; a simple distinction, so far as bullets were concerned.

We took counsel over breakfast. The sergeant in command of the local detachment told us cynically enough that we would be better off without his escort—we must change our republican sashes and cockades before starting. Fromond, who knew the country, proposed that we take the hill road via La Bec.

"Good!" exclaimed Kerguelec promptly. "It will not be watched for travellers, and I can guide you. What do you think, sergeant?"

The latter shrugged. "Your Breton garb will help, citizen! At the same time, who knows? we have spies everywhere among us. Even now perhaps word has gone out. The church bells, such as remain, send messages; smoke-signals go up. These accursed Whites have the guile of the devil! And let them learn that Citizen Fromond is on the road—pouf!"

"Good!" said Tronchet, with a huge laugh. "If

ONE IS NOT ALONE

we meet Jean Chouan, then Fromond is our prisoner!"

"And if necessary we may have to shoot him," added Rabaut maliciously. Fromond snarled at this. "For the good of the Republic of course," said Rabaut. "Well, comrades, let's change our colors and be off! We'll trust to Kerguelec's tongue."

We mounted and rode.

Both Fromond and Kerguelec knew the roads, and it seemed that our anxiety had been all vain, for we rode half the morning through the wooded Norman hills without encountering a living soul. There were evidences of the dead, however. A rising flight of birds drew us a few yards off the road, where we found the bodies of a dozen Paris volunteers, arms tied behind their backs, lying in a row upon the chenille moss. Only this, and trampled brush, and silence.

We rode on. These thickets of oak and beech and bramble might hide an army anywhere. The road was rough, and the only vestige of habitation we struck was a burned hut with the corpses of two women and a child, recently bayoneted, lying before it; a heart-chilling indication of the manner of this warfare.

97

SAINT MICHAEL'S GOLD

Men were here, invisible, in this wilderness—detached parties of grenadiers or scouts, entire battalions, wild ragged peasants by hundreds all lost to sight. It was toward noon that we distinctly heard half a dozen regular volleys, somewhere to the south of us, followed by a furious crackling fusillade. Another volley, weaker this time, and a third, drowned in a final rattle of musketry. Rabaut looked off among the trees and pinched snuff.

"More volunteers from Paris needed," he observed with cold cynicism.

We halted briefly at noon to dine on the provisions and wine fetched from Mortain. Tronchet bore his huge sheathed sword across his shoulders, though awkwardly, and refused to lay aside the weapon; it was his wife, he said laughingly. During the meal, Fromond eagerly proposed putting him to use at Mont St. Michel.

"The place is crammed with prisoners," he informed us. "Old and sick priests. The Bastille of Paris was destroyed—the Bastille of the ocean has been put to use. Since the devil has sent us a headsman, why not use him? It will be an excellent thing for the morale of the soldiers there, if they see a few priests executed."

"An excellent idea," approved Rabaut, half in

ONE IS NOT ALONE

jest. I saw Tronchet give Citizen Fromond a queer sidelong glance, and if ever savage enmity flashed in a man's eyes, it did then. I wondered.

When we again mounted, we were forced to draw rein, almost at once, in some consternation. My horse had unaccountably gone lame. Kerguelec's beast, bandaged above the fetlock by reason of a slight wound, had also become so lame as scarce to set foot to the ground. To get any fresh mounts was impossible, and Rabaut had no mind to be lingering on this road. Fromond too was furious—he had most reason to fear this stage of the journey. I gave Kerguelec a look and caught a demure wink.

"Well, well, let's divide!" cried out Tronchet cheerfully. "Citizen Fromond knows the road— you ride on with him, Citizen Rabaut! I have some skill with horses, and in half an hour I can get these two beasts fit for the road. We'll limp along after you and get into Avranches sometime tonight. Or let Citizen Martin take my horse and go on with you—"

Rabaut was no fool. He might have scented something amiss here, had it not been for the procureur. Fromont erupted in a savage burst of fear and anger, demanding that Rabaut ride on with him, and I yielded to it, refusing to take Tronchet's horse.

"Go ahead, Rabaut—it's the best plan," I said. "Fromond can guide you, and two men with white cockades will not be molested. If you do meet anyone, tell them we're following, and wait for Kerguelec to pull you out of the fire."

Rabaut nodded. "Come along as best you can, then. I'll send out a detachment to meet you. Good luck!"

He rode off with Fromond and they disappeared along the winding hill track. Once they were out of sight, I turned to Tronchet and Kerguelec, who were looking over the horses.

"Well," I said drily, "since you know so much, Tronchet, suppose you tell me the reason for this sudden lameness?"

"The hill roads." Laughing, he held up a stone he had prised from the hoof of my horse. "Since you want the truth, have it! Rid your poor beast of pain, Kerguelec."

With a slight smile, the Breton loosened the bandage about the fetlock of his mount, and I perceived it had been drawn supremely tight, with a ligature beneath. At once the horse was relieved.

ONE IS NOT ALONE

"What the devil does all this mean?" I demanded angrily.

Kerguelec made a gesture of caution, his frowning gaze on Tronchet. The latter, however, came to me and laid a hand on my arm with a broad grin.

"Look you, citizen!" he said, assuming an air of frankness. "Kerguelec made a little plot, and I fell in with it. He is wise, this Breton! Who are those two men just departed? Why, Fromond and Rabaut! If we meet anyone of the countryside, Fromond certainly will be known. Their company would be our death-warrant. We three, not being famous men, can now ride along comfortably and without fear."

Plausible enough, certainly, yet I sniffed a good deal more in it than this. Then, from behind Tronchet, Kerguelec repeated his gesture of caution, this time more emphatically. I yielded.

"Very well, Tronchet. Ride ahead. I want to speak with Kerguelec."

Tronchet nodded, laughed, and broke into a droll story guaranteed to bring blushes to the cheek of M. de Voltaire. I cut him short in apparent ill-humor, and we mounted. Although the animals limped a trifle, they were sound enough for the road. Tronchet took the lead, and once he was beyond earshot, Kerguelec leaned over and spoke sharply.

"Beware of that man!"

"Why?" I asked. The Breton shrugged.

"I don't know, but he's not what he seems. For a headsman, there's something strange about him. He may be a spy—may be anything! It was not my scheme to lame the horses, but his own, and I fell in with it because it suited me. He tried to borrow one of my pistols, and I refused. It's all very curious."

I nodded thoughtfully. Our big Tronchet had some game in hand; if, for example, he were a robber, he had managed things quite well to get me and Kerguelec alone. Then I turned and met the dark gaze of the Breton.

"And why did you fall in with his scheme, then?"

"In order to have a talk with you."

"Devil take you!" I checked myself. "Pardon; I forgot you were a woman, for the moment. I want none of your plots or missions, and this is not the time to leave Rabaut. If you want to get away, you're free to go, and the bocage will welcome you. I can't slip into the brush, however—I want to get out of the country."

"Good. I'm one with you there," said Kerguelec

promptly. "I'm not leaving Rabaut, but I must have speech with you. We're all bound for Mont St. Michel. I have private affairs there, of supreme importance to me—"

I broke in curtly, even angrily.

"Will you cease your everlasting efforts to drag me into your intrigues? Understand once and for all, I want nothing to do with them!"

Kerguelec regarded me with a little smile.

"Very well. Remember your words later on— you may be sorry, my friend! I know you are my friend, despite your rough speech. You refuse my private affairs—so be it! Yet I, too, have an errand in regard to that treasure."

"Eh?" Surprise bore down my anger at his insistance. "The treasure?"

"Exactly. The cause has need of it, for it's enormous. If I can't get away with it, I must prevent it going to Paris. However, I had hoped the two of us might turn the trick. With a little boldness, we could secure it and slip away in a boat. From the mount to the open sea, the whole length of the bay of Cancale, is no short distance—yet it might be done."

"Impossible," I returned, resigned to the discussion. The clever rascal had tricked me into it rather neatly. "The whole coast is under watch and guard. Not even a fishing boat can slip out through the French fleet."

"Except with luck and a seaman to aid," said Kerguelec, "and I have some hope of finding the seaman to aid us. A bold man can achieve the impossible, and this is not so impossible as it seems. Believe me, I've thought it over many times, have made plans. You'll not be angry if I tell you briefly what might be done?"

Kerguelec spoke rapidly, earnestly. I listened in amazement to find the details of his plan leaping at me ready prepared and thought out, presented to me as feasible.

"A dozen fishermen-militia hold the place —enough to defend it against an army, though their only duty is to guard the prisoners. Once admitted with Rabaut, we can bide our time to put Rabaut out of the way. Then take the treasure and go, especially if we find a seaman among the prisoners to aid us. I can arrange for bands of peasants to surround Dol, Pontorson and other nearby towns, keeping the Blues engaged. If we desire, some of the priests can be set free and they'll help us—"

I broke in with a laugh, half of admiration.

"Faith, you could seize the place and be done with it! No. It's out of the question."

"Why?" he demanded earnestly. "Have you no regard for what this gold might do, once the princes had it in their hands?"

"Not a snap," I said with frankness. "I don't give a turn of my hand for your princes, and would not trouble myself to help them. Indeed, I came to France to help against them!"

"But have you no regard for the English, your own blood?"

"When I fought against them as a boy for freedom? Not a scrap!"

"Is there anything for which you have regard?" he demanded with hot disappointed anger.

"Yes," I said bluntly. "Myself and my own safety."

"Very well! A share of this treasure, then, shall go to you—"

"Having regard for myself, I am not for sale."

The Breton was silent an instant. Then came the voice, not of Kerguelec, but of Marie de Rohan, low and pleading.

"Monsieur, if I appeal to you as a woman—"

"The title of monsieur is banned under penalty of death," I broke in coldly. "The only appeal you

105

can make to me, as a woman, is to help you secure your own safety. So far, I am bound. For the gold —no!"

Kerguelec muttered something under his breath that sounded suspiciously like an oath and I chuckled. Then I looked up sharply. We had been winding up a half-clad, barren hillock, and Tronchet's voice reached us. He had drawn rein and was waiting, pointing back.

"Look! Name of the Black Man, are we pursued?"

I glanced around. Below we could see snatches of the rough track as it wound, and spurts of dust were going up in the hot sunlight. I gazed narrowly.

"Two men only," I said. "Horsemen, riding hard."

"Tricolored sashes," added Kerguelec.

I got out my pistols and primed them, for they were already fresh loaded. Tronchet fumbled beneath his coat, produced a pistol, and asked me for fresh priming from my flask.

"So!" exclaimed Kerguelec. "You were very anxious to borrow a pistol from me this morning, Citizen Tronchet!"

"Of course," returned Tronchet coolly. "Having but one, I wanted two. But why do we get out

ONE IS NOT ALONE

pistols, citizen assistant commissaire, for men wearing our own colors?"

"That," I said curtly, "remains to be seen. Ride on."

I was suspicious of the man now, in view of what Kerguelec had said, and did not doubt he had meant to kill us both and rob us if possible, incredible as such a scheme might seem. However, I had other things to bother with at present, being alarmed by the appearance of the two horsemen a half-mile behind us. They must have secured fresh mounts at Mortain and had there learned of our passing. It argued they were in mad haste to catch up with Rabaut—and boded no good to me.

We were all thinking more of the men behind than of anyone ahead. So, ten minutes later when we came upon the first living creatures we had encountered all day, we were all three somewhat startled. The meeting was abrupt, without warning, as we broke into an open glade where a brook crossed the road and the brush was thick all around.

There before us in the center of the opening, wide-eyed in alarm at our sudden appearance, was a peasant. He was a brutish, gnarled, wild fellow, holding over his shoulder an ominously stained pitchfork, and in his other hand a rope. Upon this rope staggered behind him a horrible figure—a man, half naked, smeared with blood and dirt, eyes shut with blood coming from a wound across his head.

The peasant jerked on his rope, halting the captive. Greenery closed in the spot like a wall, the sun beat down hotly. The miserable prisoner went to his knees, head hanging in utter exhaustion. I dismounted and the peasant, though obviously alarmed, faced me boldly enough—he had no escape. He was a most villainous rascal.

"Well, citizens?" he snarled. "Who are you, with white sashes? Whites never ride horses!"

"I am a commissioner from Paris," I said, knowing from his language he was a Blue.

He grinned at this. "Ha! Well met, citizen— anybody would know you were not Whites! Why, I am Citizen Leclerc, whose farm lies half a mile north, and I have caught a ci-devant, an émigré! Look at him—pretty, the aristocrat! Rather, I caught two, an old one and this young one. My pitchfork did for the old one; he was a sick rascal, not worth troubling with. I'm taking the young one to Avranches to see him shot. If Citizen Fromond is there, I may get a reward."

"Citizen Fromond has passed on this road not

twenty minutes ago," I said. The peasant rubbed his chin.

"Ah! If I had known that, eh? Too bad I killed the old one; Fromond would have given a reward for the team, certainly. However, he died like a pig—"

He broke into horrible laughter. There was a queer sound behind, and I looked around to see Kerguelec and Tronchet dismounted and coming forward. Tronchet was staggering like a man drunk, and his face, though pallid as death, was streaming with sweat.

"What's the matter, man!" I exclaimed.

"The heat, the heat," he mumbled. I laughed lightly.

"Well, here's a chance to earn your first ten francs. Get out your sword and go to work!"

"You—you mean it?" he asked hoarsely. "On this prisoner?"

"Certainly," I said, and cocked my pistol. "It is an order."

"Very well, citizen commissioner," he blurted, wiping the sweat from his face.

The prisoner, apparently a young man, drooped in the hot sun. The peasant gaped at me open-mouthed. I met Kerguelec's eyes and caught a gesture of protesting incredulity, returning a nod of reassurance. I had taken the whim to test out Citizen Tronchet a little. The man knew me only as assistant commissioner, of course, and Kerguelec as a Breton serving Rabaut; and having made up my mind to put a bullet into this murderous peasant, I wanted first to see where our headsman stood.

As executioner, something certainly was amiss with him. He seemed to utter a low groan as he drew the great sword from its shoulder-bandolier with fumbling hands, and wet his lips. He tried to draw the blade free, but it stuck a little. A wild oath burst from him. He lifted the sword in both hands and sent it hurling away through the air. Then he jerked at his pistol, strode forward a pace, and looked at the peasant. His face was convulsed.

"You killed the old man with your fork, did you?" he asked.

"Aye!" The peasant grimaced. "He died hard, I can tell you! These cursed aristocrats hang on to life like cats. But I finished him."

"He was my father," cried out Tronchet, "and this man is my brother—"

On the word, he jerked up his pistol. The report bellowed, white smoke belched. The peasant whirled around and fell in a huddled heap. It was done all in a flash, swiftly.

Tronchet gave a leap, reached the side of the captive, and flung an arm about the red-naked shoulders. He turned, facing me and Kerguelec, and the man was transformed; every vestige of the Tronchet we knew was gone. He stood holding his empty pistol; a sudden calm settled upon him, a certain indescribable majesty showed in his face.

"I am Vicomte de Chaponay. Now do your worst, you devils of Paris!"

A ci-devant, an émigré, hiding as executioner! Now I saw everything—he had not planned to rob us, but to make his escape from us, and admiration leaped in me. With a gesture, I checked a sudden movement from Kerguelec. Something warned me, thrilled me. All around us in the brush was a rustle, as though something moved in the bocage.

"Tronchet, go pick up your sword," I said. He flung a terrible look at me, his eyes tortured. Then the shadow of his gay laugh reached me.

"The sword? Bah! I bought it in a shop. I fled one way, my father and brother the other. We've all failed—finish it! Vive le Roi!"

"Don't be a fool," I said. "I've no intention of —ah!"

SAINT MICHAEL'S GOLD

I turned, for in upon us sounded a trampling of hooves. Breaking suddenly into the glade, as we ourselves had done, came two horsemen, those who had been riding after us. From their attire, they were couriers. Reining in their sweat-lathered beasts, they seized pistols, at sight of our white sashes and cockades. I called to them hastily.

"Ho, citizens! You seek Citizen Rabaut?"

"Aye," exclaimed one, in obvious relief at this form of address. "We have important news—orders for the arrest of his assistant, Citizen Martin, a traitor——"

"You've told that to the wrong man," I said, and fired.

The first reeled in his saddle and fell heavily. The second had taken warning. He whirled his horse around, spurring hard, and my second pistol missed him. Kerguelec fired, missed likewise. With a yell and a great leap, he was going in a burst of speed.

I ran forward to the dead man, searched him hastily. Nothing! The second, then, had carried the despatches. For an instant I thought of pursuing him, but already too much time had been wasted. He could slip into the brush and elude me too easily.

ONE IS NOT ALONE

I rose and came back to the others, looking at the stupified, staring Tronchet.

"I'm sorry!" said Kerguelec contritely. "If I had not missed him—"

"No matter," I said. "He'll return to Mortain and go the other way around to Avranches. He may wait for an escort of Blues. We'll be two or three days ahead of him at least."

A cry of amazement burst from Tronchet.

"Name of the devil! What does this mean? You, a commissioner from Paris——"

"I'm a fugitive from Paris," I said, "and those two men bore orders for my arrest. As for our Breton friend here, I've another surprise for you. We're all in the same boat."

Kerguelec swept off his wide Breton hat and uttered a laugh.

"So, M. de Chaponay! I have the honor to salute you."

"And who the devil are you?" he demanded.

"Mademoiselle de Rohan," I said, laughing a little.

"Marie de Rohan," amended Kerguelec, "and I believe distantly connected with your house, M. de Chaponay."

From Tronchet came one astounded exclamation; his expression was dismayed, ludicrous, and he stood there with his jaw hanging, utterly aghast. In this moment he must have recalled those droll stories he had been recounting on the road, the excellence with which he had played at his rôle of headsman. Then all three of us broke into sudden laughter.

From this I was startled by a sound in the brush, the crackle of a dead stick. The ominous noise wakened me. I ran to the fallen man and jerked out his unused pistols.

"Too much talk!" I called sharply. "Quick, Tronchet—look alive! Someone nearby——"

On the word, the bocage around us seemed to be swept by motion. A man appeared. Other men flooded into the glade from all sides. The barren rocks sprouted muskets, the very trees broke into movement, showed men lying in the branches or dropping to earth.

Strangely enough, not a word was spoken. Silent, they came pouring in upon us from all directions, as we stood there petrified—men armed with muskets, with pikes, with sabers string-tied to belts, with staves and scythes—men ragged and unkempt, barefoot or shod with leathern gaiters, nearly all having flaming hearts broidered on their tattered jackets—bearded, long-haired, shaggy men.

They closed us within a human wall, still in this unreal silence, their wild eyes fastened upon us. Suddenly they opened out, to let one man pass through them to the center. He was short, sturdy, bronzed, with commanding features, and his gaze was directed at me with anger.

"You did wrong!" he exclaimed abruptly. "Had you not killed that rascal we should have had them both! You spoiled my trap, monsieur, and I don't thank you for it!"

I was too amazed to make response.

CHAPTER VI

ONE TRUSTS, ANOTHER CONFIDES

THE leader of our rescuers or captors, as the case might prove, turned from me to Kerguelec. He removed his wide hat in peasant fashion, and spoke awkwardly. He had a distinct Breton brogue.

"Mademoiselle, princess, you are safe. We heard all. Be assured."

There was a stir. His men were freeing and caring for the unhappy captive, who was now clinging to Tronchet. The two brothers embraced warmly. The man from the bocage put a hand on Tronchet's arm and smiled.

"Well met, monsieur! I hoped our men might pick you up—I heard of your escape." He crossed himself quickly. "Your father—may he rest in peace!—is gone. You and your brother remain. M. de la Rochejacquelin will be glad of your help. Do you know we have forty thousand men? It is true.

116

ONE TRUSTS, ANOTHER CONFIDES

We have soundly whipped the Blues at Fontenay. I am here on a swift errand, to create a diversion and return south immediately. We have little time to talk—four miles from here there is a detachment of Blues, cornered and held until we come. We pause only to destroy them, then back to the Vendée before we are caught and trapped."

He turned his steady, piercing eyes to me. "Who are you, monsieur? Your actions have spoken for you, but your name——"

"Martin," I said. "I am an American, a member of the convention. Marat tried to take my head, and I kept it."

My light tone did not draw even a smile. There was no mirth in these men. When I spoke of belonging to the convention, a low breath passed around, a growl; hands tightened on weapons. Then Kerguelec spoke out, eagerly.

"Do not harm him! He has been in Paris, helping many of us away to safety. He is not of our party, yet time and again he has risked his life for us. He saved me from the guillotine. He saved Madame de Florelle and her children. Comte d'Artois has given him nobility——"

The man before me suddenly went to his knees. Before I realized his intention, he seized my hand

and pressed it to his lips. He rose, and I saw the glitter of tears in his eyes.

"Ah, monsieur—you, an American do this!" he exclaimed. A wild roar of applause went up from the ragged crew all around, pikes and musket-butts thudded on the ground. "Monsieur, I am only a peasant, a carter, humble before you. I salute you."

"Your name, monsieur?" I asked curiously.

"Jacques Cathelineau."

Cathelineau! The name drew a start from me— of late it had resounded largely in Paris, was being uttered through half of France, had become known in England and Germany. Before me stood the most dreaded guerilla leader of the Vendéan insurrection, the man once no better than a serf, now one of the chief props on which leaned the princes of the house of Bourbon.

Paris thought the name of the dead king was Capet, though it was nothing of the sort. And Paris thought this man of the west was a mere peasant carter, whom the renegade nobles would crush with their thousands of volunteers. Paris was very liable to mistakes those days!

Suddenly a voice broke in upon the scene, an eager panting voice. A man hurled himself out of the thickets, burst a way through the surrounding throng, came to a stop before us.

"Jacques!" he broke forth eagerly, in a dialect I could scarce understand. "Two wagons coming from Avranches——fifty Blues! Not half a mile away—along this road—heading for Mortain—"

Cathelineau whirled, and into his face leaped savage exultation.

"Ready! Where are you, father?"

What now took place was swift and remarkable in its silence, for I did not hear so much as an order given. The sense of unreality was stunning. This astonishing meeting with Jacques Cathelineau and his men of the bocage, presumably a hundred miles away, and the whirlwind drama of the following events still remain with me like a dream. Despite all I knew, had seen, had heard, it was hard to credit such warfare in Europe.

Cathelineau lifted his hand, and a priest in tattered, tucked-up cassock made his appearance. The whole company went to their knees while the priest, as I gathered, gave absolution and made a short prayer; the savage faces around me became devout, intent, rapt. Then everyone leaped into action.

What became of the others, I hardly realized— they seemed to melt away and vanish. Cathelineau took my arm, and I found myself accompanying him; we were alone, striding hurriedly through the forest. He noted my pace, my ability to thread the heavy undergrowth, and smiled.

"You have followed the wood trails ere this, eh? Well, you shall have something to tell them in America," he said grimly.

He led me a stiff pace, and I had no time to exchange words. The thicket of brush had apparently swallowed everyone else; we two were alone, Cathelineau leading the way as though he could see beyond the enclosing trees.

Ten minutes of this; then, breathing hard, I came to a halt at his side. Before us in the afternoon sunlight lay an open stretch of the road, with rising ground on either side dotted with sparse growth of beech and oak.

At the far end of this visible road, a group of dragoons was riding toward us, ten mounted men, muskets ready, jogging along easily enough and without thought of danger. Behind them came into sight two lumbering, creaking wagons, followed again by another two-score of men. These were from a Parisian regiment, ragged, enthusiastic volunteers, whose appearance contrasted strongly with the gay brass and plumes of the dragoon vanguard. I glanced along the hillside to either hand, but could see no one.

"Where are your men?" I muttered to Cathelineau. His only response was a slow, terrible smile.

The wagons creaked forward until they were but thirty yards away from us, directly in the center of the open stretch. The dragoons were even closer upon us, though somewhat below. And of a sudden Cathelineau lifted his voice in one powerful shout.

"Vive le Roi!"

A signal, I thought—but no! Nothing moved in the bocage. Startled shouts arose from the dragoons and the soldiers. The vanguard drew rein and clattered back to the wagons, which had halted. Off to the right on the hillside appeared a dozen ragged figures, who gave a scattering discharge of muskets. Two of the dragoons went down.

Orders cracked out, drums rolled. A vivandière, perched on one of the wagons, slapped her canteen and shrilled Parisian argot at the soldiers. The infantry lined up, facing the right, where the ragged figures had increased to a score in number, gathering as though to charge down and exposing themselves boldly. Coolly ranked, the soldiers lifted their muskets. A volley of smoke and flame erupted.

Yet, as the word sounded to fire, the peasants

vanished from sight, flinging themselves down while the bullets whistled above them. Then, from both sides of the road, burst out a wild roar of voices. Instantly the volley was fired, a torrent of men rose from tree and bush, poured forward, hurled itself down headlong upon the road. Cathelineau left my side and was in among the first, rusty saber in hand.

Their muskets empty, the soldiers fixed bayonets and attempted to meet the mad charge. They might as well have tried to stem a torrent of water with a basket.

They were caught behind and before. Bullets rained in upon them. The eddying smoke glinted to sun-gleams of sabers and long scythes; I saw of it all only one incident, the vivandière leaping down from her wagon to be impaled upon a pike, half a dozen others pinning her to the earth as she fell. In fifteen seconds the ranks were broken, in thirty, half the Blues were dead. Before a minute had passed, not half a dozen soldiers kept their feet, and around them surged the peasants with the ferocity of wolves.

I ran forward. As I came to the wagons, the last republican went down—an officer, sabered by Cathelineau in person. As I reached the side of the guerilla leader, a man rushed up to us exultantly.

"Finished!"

"The prisoners?" demanded Cathelineau.

"There are none."

"Good. The wagons are loaded with powder. Set fire to them. Save horses for our friends here. Scatter the others in the bocage. Ready to march!"

I remembered now how Cathelineau had spoken of a detachment of soldiers cornered and kept penned against his coming. Bloody work, this!

The thing held me dazed, stupefied. I saw the ragged priest moving around among the dying, while the wounded peasants were being lifted and borne off. The horses were being quieted, the wagons explored. As I stood there helplessly, Tronchet came up to me, a black powder-smear across his face, and gripped my hand.

"Farewell!" he exclaimed. "I'm off to the Vendée, with my brother. You played your part too well, Monsieur American—you fooled me completely!"

"The same to you," I returned.

"God guard you!" he said, and he was gone.

Cathelineau and Kerguelec came toward me, the latter speaking earnestly.

"No," I heard him say. "No, I must go on. I

have my own errands to do. Monsieur Martin goes with me—or I with him."

Cathelineau gave me a look of inquiry, and I nodded.

"Yes. I'm not of your party, or of any party—I go to America. If I join you, my chance of reaching the sea is gone. But you can still help me, if you will! That courier who escaped, bore orders for my arrest——"

"I have already issued instructions," said Cathelineau. "I must get away at once, as soon as we finish the other detachment of Blues, but I have sent out a few men. If the courier reaches Avranches, it will be a miracle."

"Miracles happen," I said. He crossed himself and gave me a stern glance, not liking my tone of voice.

"They can happen for as well as against, monsieur." He dropped to one knee and brought Kerguelec's hand to his lips. "Mademoiselle, I have horses here, ready for you. Take them and get away at once. You need not hesitate to speak of me—before the Blues get after me, I'll be far away! Farewell, with God!"

Five minutes afterward, mounted on dragoon horses, we were riding away westward. In another five, the whole scene was gone and we two were alone in the forest, Kerguelec and I.

For a time we rode in silence. Glancing back I saw a thick column of smoke rising, and presently we caught the thunderous reverberation of the explosion, making our horses leap. I was heavily oppressed by the happenings—by the incredible rapidity of all we had witnessed. From the time we glimpsed the peasant and his haltered captive, scarce half an hour could have elapsed; yet what had taken place in this short time! Against such foes, no wonder the regular officers and generals found the Vendean war confusing, bewildering, hopeless!

I looked at Kerguelec suddenly. "If Cathelineau had known—about Rabaut!"

"He knows, but cannot wait now to catch him," said the Breton gravely. "He must get off to the south tonight. However, Rabaut still has enemies."

"Ah!" A significance in the tone caught my attention. "Is that woman's work?"

"You are a man."

I leaned over and put my hand on his firm, slender fingers.

"Listen, my dear girl!" I said earnestly. "Will you not give up your ideas of using me? I am not a man to be used, I assure you."

125

SAINT MICHAEL'S GOLD

"You mistake." Kerguelec rested a steady gaze on me. "You must ultimately get rid of Rabaut, not for my ends, but for your own. You've refused the mission I offered you—very well. You've refused to help me in my private errand. No more appeals! I'm competent to carry out my own work. As for the treasure, if I cannot get the gold I shall prevent it going to Paris. Are you satisfied?"

"Entirely," I said. A sudden ringing laugh broke from the Breton.

"How bewildered you looked, back there! It was remarkable about Tronchet. I never suspected him —how wonderful it all seems, now! What shall you tell Rabaut, when we show up without Tronchet?"

"The truth," I said shortly. Kerguelec gave me a glance, but said no more.

I was not courteous in the extreme, true, yet this came rather from an excess of care on my own part, an endeavor to treat Kerguelec exactly like the man he seemed. That a girl of high family should play such a part, especially a French girl, was a thing unheard-of; it bespoke acute emergency, and I regretted having refused to listen to any talk of private affairs in my anxiety to keep clear of public matters. How much Kerguelec must have gone

ONE TRUSTS, ANOTHER CONFIDES

through in playing this rôle I could well understand. Above all, I was horribly afraid for him. A word, a gesture, a trick of expression might betray him at any instant, for already Rabaut had discovered something familiar in his face.

As we rode, the remembrance of what we had just witnessed lingered deeply with us—less so with me perhaps than with Kerguelec. It was not my country run rabid with civil war, they were not my people and kinsfolk who destroyed each other like wild beasts. Despite all we had seen, it was very hard, in this warm flooding afternoon sunlight, to realize the terrific disruption of France—to credit the butchery going on to the south of us, to feel that a hundred thousand men were already in arms to repress this western rebellion, and were failing in the effort!

A league from the hill of Avranches, we came down into a village and the main highway. Scarcely were we through the village, when ahead of us sounded a roaring chorus of voices, thundering out an air we both recognized—the battle-hymn of the revolution, to which the children danced in the streets of Paris:

"Ah, ça ira, ça ira, ça ira,
Les aristocrats à la lanterne!"

127

SAINT MICHAEL'S GOLD

We drew rein and waited. It brought back everything to me—even those "lanterns" or street lamps of Paris, with the large square hook at the top, where many a poor devil had found an improvised gibbet! And so there broke upon us a score of mounted dragoons, who flooded about us, stared at me, stared at the strange Breton figure, until an officer pushed forward and demanded our names. I gave them.

"Good!" he exclaimed. "We were sent out to meet and escort you, citizens!" He looked at Kerguelec curiously, for his regiment was newly arrived in the west. "So this is a Breton, eh? What a savage! I never saw a Breton before—"

"But I have seen these horses before!" shouted a sergeant, pointing excitedly to our mounts. "Devil take me if that isn't Jambe d'Argent's horse and saddle!"

Shouts, oaths, questions, further recognition. I beckoned the officer.

"To Avranches, at once—hush up these fools! I have news for Citizen Rabaut."

He obtained order. I passed the word that I had been halted by Whites, who had destroyed the convoy of powder, but had gained clear of them by Kerguelec's help. Amid new oaths and vows of vengeance for their slain comrades, the soldiers turned about and we all rode forward to the town on the hill, above the wide bay of Cancale.

It was drawing on to sunset when we mounted the heights to the quarters of Rabaut—a building opposite a huge mass of ruins, in the front of them a single broken pillar bearing a plate of brass. The town was filled with troops; they were quartered on the houses, were bivouacked in the streets, were crowding everywhere. General Wimpfen, commanding the La Manche army in this district, had been here only a week previously and had left a strong garrison behind him.

We found Rabaut in a large room, surrounded by members of the local committee and a number of officers. At sight of us, Rabaut leaped up with unwonted effusiveness, came forward, and embraced me with warmth.

"Not a word of our errand!" he murmured as he flung his arms about me. Then, louder; "All well? You came through safely? But where is Tronchet?"

"Dead," I responded with perfect truth. Rabaut drew back, and there was a general stir of interest.

"Dead? Then you met Whites?"

"None," I replied drily, "except Cathelineau and

some hundreds of his peasants. They had just cut off a convoy and two wagons. Tronchet is dead. Thanks to Kerguelec, who has proven his worth to us this day, we secured a couple of horses and got away."

Instantly the room was in mad uproar. The loss of convoy and powder was nothing, but the bare name of Cathelineau unloosed a tide of wild confusion and panic. There was no idea of ordering out troops after the guerilla—everyone leaped into fear that the guerilla would be before the gates of Avranches. The first fear was succeeded by stupefaction, for the proximity of the dreaded rebel was incredible. When I assured them Cathelineau was already on his way back to the Vendée, relief was swift, and Kerguelec came in for loud applause.

Under cover of the uproar, Rabaut spoke quietly in my ear.

"Not a room in this cursed place is safe. Go across to the ruins of the cathedral, and I'll join you presently."

"Quarters first," I said. "We're both dust-covered, and I'm loaded with everything from pistols to comb."

I so spoke for Kerguelec's sake, and it proved Fromond had offered quarters in his own house to the Breton—luckily enough, since space in the town was at a premium. So we parted, and I was conducted to the room I shared with Rabaut in this same building.

In another fifteen minutes, I left the place and sauntered across to the ruins. By questioning a citizen, I learned the cathedral had abruptly fallen of its own age, three years previously—helped somewhat by Citizen Fromond, no doubt. This was not surprising, considering it was over seven hundred years old.

Of this age, indeed, I was given unique and startling proof when I approached the broken pillar, formerly on the porch of the cathedral. The old brass plate affixed to it bore characters still legible, informing me that upon this spot Henry II of England had received absolution for the murder of Thomas à Becket, in the year 1172. I wondered what the old king would think of his French duchy nowadays, if he could see it!

The sun was sinking to rest when Rabaut approached me, coolly enough.

"Your news has raised the devil again, just as I had things calmed down," he said with a laugh. "I've arrested a colonel, approved a dozen denunciations, and have ordered a rascally renegade priest shot in the morning. I think these fools are now convinced of my authority. Too bad about Tronchet—I liked the rogue. Martin, we must ride in the morning."

"Good. What about an immediate dinner?"

"We dine with Fromond in half an hour. How many dragoons do you want to take along to the Mont, as escort?"

"That depends. Rabaut, you'll have to put your cards on the table," I said, and met his insolent, sharply-inquiring eyes firmly. "For our own safety, we need only Kerguelec. For the sake of appearances—"

"In the eyes of Fromond," he added, and took a pinch of snuff. "Right. Damn Fromond! He and the jeweler ride with us. I appear to have had a narrow escape today from Cathalineau, eh? Are you certain it was the man himself—"

"One thing at a time," I interrupted curtly. "Cards down, Rabaut, if we're to reach any agreement!"

For a long moment he regarded me fixedly, queer menacing glints showing in those dark eyes of his. Then, fingering his snuffbox, he turned and stared at the street.

Rabaut was in the valley of decision. Until this

moment, I now perceived, he had been entertaining temptation half-heartedly, and now he must decide once and for all, for or against. If he came out into the open and trusted me with his rascality, there could be no retreat for him.

"It's a devilish well-guarded affair," he reflected, half to me, half to himself. "The jeweler is to weigh the stuff on the spot, while I check off the items on the inventory with Fromond. We fetch everything back here, turn it over to the jeweler, who then hands me the money for the metal. You comprehend?"

He gave me a steady look. Cold-blooded rogue as he was, he yet needed a prod. I gave it without compunction, since I had no pity for him.

"Yes," I said and nodded. "Yes. Once we return here, the chance is gone. Come, speak out! Is that it or not? Trust me or else lose all the wager."

He snapped his snuffbox shut and plunged.

"That's it. We must get the treasure at the Mont, or nowhere. Do we take the chance, you and I?"

"For what—for the gold?" I demanded relentlessly.

"The gold and the future. All of life! My

133

authority extends to St. Malo, the limit of this district. Say the word, and I can send off a letter tonight to that town, ordering a lugger to meet us off Mont St. Michel in three days. You and I, between us, manage the affair. We get a boat at the Mont, load the gold into it, and get away—that's it, roughly."

He watched me closely, to see how I would receive this bald proposition.

"All well and good, as far as you go," I returned. "At all events, we're to be no petty thieves!"

"Petty?" Warmth crept into his voice. "Martin, I've seen the inventory—the gold alone in that place is worth a king's ransom! Half of it would suffice a dozen men for life."

"We go halves?" I demanded.

"Halves. Your objection to my scheme?"

"None, so far as it goes," I reflected. "But what comes after? You cannot land with it in England, or it will be seized for the royalist cause. There's a French fleet off the coast, and all the bay is watched. Go—whither?"

He laughed softly, for once with genuine amusement.

"To America, blind one! You forgot how much power a commissioner has! The lugger meets us

ONE TRUSTS, ANOTHER CONFIDES

—I give the orders. If any republican frigate stops us, we go to America on a mission from the convention. Vive la République! Liberty, equality, fraternity, and the rights of man! It is simple, if one has the password," he added cynically.

"Simple and reasonably safe," I responded thoughtfully. "We might get past the fleet, after all—it's bold enough to work! Our only risk comes from the sea, then, and from an English ship."

"Not from the sea in summer!" countered Rabaut quickly. "These luggers are safe as a three-decker, and too small to be bothered by the English. Even if stopped, we are fishermen bound for the Newfoundland banks, or émigrés—not worth bothering."

"Devilish bold, simple and ingenious," I observed admiringly.

"Like all great plans." Rabaut tapped his snuff-box, and fixed his eyes upon me. "But what assurance have I of your coöperation, Martin? Or, in exact terms, that you'll not betray me to Fromond?"

I laughed a little. "A most excellent assurance, my good citizen! The fact that Marat wants my head."

"Eh?" He started, his gaze widened a trifle. "Is this true?"

135

"True." And now, under the spur of necessity, I did a very foolish thing. Not until later did I realize how my words put me in Rabaut's power. "My commission as your assistant was made out in another name. Having to flee at once, I took a long chance and won. What's more to the point, orders are out for my arrest, and I think you've been recalled."

These last words sharply swept him from my case to his own. He became piercing, alert, dangerous. I told him of the two couriers, hinting at more than I said in order to impress upon him the idea of his own possible recall. He nodded decisively.

"Good. We must not lose a moment. Then it's agreed?"

"Agreed. However, you had better keep your eye on Fromond," I added. "He's the chief danger-point."

Rabaut showed his teeth, and a hint of venom darted in his eyes.

"Let him dare! Now, what about help? We'll need a couple of stout men, and we'll have to trust them to some extent. Gold is heavy stuff to be loaded."

"Pick out two soldiers," I returned, little guessing

136

ONE TRUSTS, ANOTHER CONFIDES

how I was to pay dearly for the advice. "The
stoutest, most fanatic republicans you can find—
preferably Parisian volunteers. Show them your
commission, offer them nothing, have them detached
on special service. If you pick the right men, they'll
help you steal Mont St. Michel itself, thinking
they're doing it for the committee in Paris, and
will guard you to America!"

"Right—an excellent notion!" Rabaut smiled
slightly and clapped me on the shoulder. "Then
it's settled, so come along to Fromond's house.
That devil will be sorry to learn of Tronchet's
death—he had wrung a half-promise out of me
that he could have six priests beheaded every day,
at the Mont. Now—by the way! Kerguelec goes
with us."

His tone of decision, of command, vaguely
startled me.

"Goes with us?" I repeated. "Well, why not?"

"Oh, nothing!" A peculiar smile crossed his
face, and it turned me cold. "But I'll ride with
our Breton to-morrow. I think we'll be good company for each other."

Somehow, somewhere, had been a gap in the
armor. Rabaut knew Kerguelec's secret.

CHAPTER VII

IN vain did I seek even the least word with Kerguelec that evening. No chance afforded itself, for Rabaut fastened upon the Breton like a leech.

He was still unwarned when we rode out of Avranches in the morning, though I fancied Rabaut's manner might have given him some hint; what was passing between them, however, I could not tell. I rode in the van with our escort, four troopers from a Rhineland regiment, sturdy Alsatians who spoke German better than French. Behind me came Rabaut and Kerguelec, followed by Fromond and the jeweler—a crafty-eyed little Norman spy. Rabaut's two specially engaged troopers brought up the rear with the baggage. They were brothers, Parisians with tremendous mustaches, from a grenadier regiment, and were known as

PERIL FROM THE PAST IS SHARPEST

Pol Rouge and Pol Noir; their actual names I never knew. They were large men, active, fiery republicans, just the sort of thick-witted enthusiasts to serve Rabaut's purpose.

As a matter of fact, we were all the finest pack of would-be thieves riding the Norman roads since the Hundred Years' War. Nominally, we were about the job of stealing for the republic a treasure belonging by all right to the Benedictines of St. Maur. Actually, it was far otherwise.

Rabaut wanted to steal the gold for himself. I stood quite ready to help him, if this would further my own escape. Kerguelec wanted to steal it for the royalist cause, who had best claim to it after the monks. Fromond wanted to steal it in order to injure the priests, since it was regarded as a sacred treasure. The jeweler intended to steal all he could in weighing the metal, and I had no doubt the scales boxed behind his saddle would give full short weight. The only strictly honest men among us were the troopers—a position apt to be insecure as that of kernels between the grindstones.

I had no more fear of the courier from Paris, or his news, even if he managed to reach us. It was true that Rabaut knew my secret, but on the other hand I knew his intentions, so we were very nicely balanced. My sole cause of present uneasiness was Kerguelec, with whom I could get no private speech. This I must put up with for the present.

The most direct way from Avranches to the Mont lay straight across the beach sands. Fromond refused to consider it, however, being in dread of quicksands and of the swift tides, saying they often came in across the leagues and leagues of flat sand with the rapidity of a horse at gallop. The temptation was strong to disregard him, with the unbroken sands running far as eye could see, but Kerguelec backed up the lawyer. So we went by way of the road, via Pontaubault, Beauvoir and Pontorson— a five-league ride in all. Little enough it seemed, at the setting out, and Fromond was calculating to get to work on the treasure in the course of the afternoon.

In view of later events, I keenly regretted having put the procureur on the scent of Rabaut, whose plans now suited my own purpose excellently. If Fromond were to block him, I too would be blocked, and I could see no better method of leaving France than that suggested by Rabaut. However, it was too late now to cry over the milk.

The day was clear, beautiful, but very hot and oppressive, and we jogged along without encountering any signs of war or other disturbance. Having in mind Cathelineau's clever stratagem in collecting and surrounding the Blues, I kept two of my four Alsatians far out in advance, but we scarce saw a soul until we rode into the little town of Pontaubault.

Here the street was rapidly deserted at sight of us, good proof of the temper of the inhabitants—but not quickly enough deserted. A gray-haired peasant was hobbling across the street ahead, when Fromond uttered a cry, drove in his spurs, and clattered wildly on in advance. He cut around in front of the old man, who halted quietly, and then waved his arm to hasten us on.

"Here we have one!" he shouted. His eyes were blazing, and excitement caused the left side of his face to twitch furiously. "Quick, Citizen Martin! Bind him!"

We rode up. The old peasant regarded us calmly, even smilingly, but said no word.

"What do you mean by this?" I demanded of Fromond. He pointed down at the old peasant with his shaking hand.

"I know him! One of these superstition-serving rascals—was deported last year! He's come back, has been hiding here—oh, I know him!"

SAINT MICHAEL'S GOLD

"Yes, my poor son, and I know you," spoke out the priest, for so he was in reality. "God forgive you, as I do, your fury! It was I who baptized you, Jacques Fromond. Do you remember that later day when you made your first communion at my hands? Do you remember how you came with your parents, all clad in white? Do you remember your vow to St. Michel, or has your poor hurt brain been trying to forget all these things—"

Fromond uttered an incoherent, bestial cry, and his eyes were horrible to see in their tortured fury. He leaned over in the saddle and struck the old man brutally across the face, so that he staggered back against the house-wall beyond. At this, I nearly forgot myself. Indeed, I had whipped out a pistol when a hand fell on my arm, and I looked into the steady eyes of Kerguelec. They sobered me.

"Bind him!" howled Fromond. "Bind him and set him against a wall and shoot him! The penalty for returned priests is death—"

"Bah! Not a bit of it," said Rabaut coolly, not displeased to balk Fromond. "If we stop for that, we may have half the countryside buzzing around us before we reach Pontorson." He took a pinch of snuff and looked down at the priest. "Come, old man! Swear that you'll deliver yourself at

PERIL FROM THE PAST IS SHARPEST

Mont St. Michel—Mont Libre, I mean—to-morrow.
You agree?"

The priest wiped blood from his mouth. "I
agree," he said, and then looked up at Fromond.
He smiled a little and raised his hand. "My poor
son! God be merciful to you."

Fromond, white as death, lifted his arm to strike
a second time, when I caught his bridle and jerked
his horse away. We rode on. Fromond hurled wild
imprecations upon all of us, until he presently fell
silent, gnawing his lip and fumbling nervously with
his reins. A curious meeting, I thought, and was
glad Kerguelec had prevented my impetuous folly.
I began to think this Fromond might be mad after
all. At least he was possessed of a devil!

The procureur was very impatient to reach our
destination, that he might begin his work; he would
have pushed us on with all speed, alleging as a fact
that from noon until one o'clock, whatever the tide,
no water surrounded Mont St. Michel. Rabaut
refused to be hurried. He intended to reach Pontorson in time for noon meat, and from there cover
the two leagues across the sands to the Mont after
the tide was low. This put Fromond into a sullen
fury, but he perforce agreed.

We went our way without further happening, except the tremendous incident of sighting our destination—a vision never to be forgotten. This broke on us half a league from Pontorson, and caused us to draw rein in silence. Even Fromond, staring from his haunted eyes, must have found the sight incredible, a touch of another world.

Before us outspread the immense horizon of sea and sand, insensibly merging together, and against it was set an enormous mass of granite, conical in shape. Where rock ended and masonry began was impossible to say. This mountain, gray-set amid yellow sands and receding tide, rose against the sky, became walls and pinnacles and elongated buttresses, culminating in the pointed belfry of the abbey. At high tide this granite cone was surrounded for league on league by ocean. Now, with the tide going out, a league of water still lay around it, and this would disappear as rapidly as it would return. That this marvelous creation was the work of human hands seemed past all reason—the thing hung there between earth and heaven in a glistening mirage, a dream-castle.

After this we passed on between orchards and barley fields, and came at last into the village of Pontorson, where a few months later the heroic Vendéan army was vainly to stem the tide of destruction rolling it under. Once a famous place, crowded with pilgrims for the Mont, the village was now a gray desolation, one inn alone open and it empty of travelers.

When we dismounted and the others trooped inside, I had chance for a short word with Kerguelec and seized it.

"Danger," I said swiftly. "You had best mount and ride for it now, comrade!"

He nodded composedly. "I know. He has recollected me."

"He told you?"

Kerguelec gave me a calm look. "Yes. He knows. He threatens no danger—rather, he threatens the worst of dangers!"

"Then, for the love of heaven, get away while we're here!"

"No. I can handle him. Besides, let well enough alone! It will help me in my private errands here— and you've refused them."

With this woman-like shot, Kerguelec turned and entered the inn.

I followed, not without a muttered oath. Here was a new complication, and it left me aghast. Perhaps Rabaut had a mind to take more than one sort of treasure along on his flight to America!

SAINT MICHAEL'S GOLD

An officer and a dozen dragoons were quartered in the town. While we were at our meal the officer appeared, both to learn our business and to get his own dinner. Sight of Rabaut's commission properly awed him, and he fell to work at his own meal in the corner. He was a veteran of fifty, a bullet-headed Norman, thick of wits, sluggish of thought, with all the slow perserverance of a bloodhound. Despite the new army formations and his obvious years of the work, it spoke eloquently for his quality that he had not risen above a captaincy—when half-baked turncoat lieutenants of the royal army now commanded brigades!

It chanced that I sat beside Kerguelec, both of us facing the table of the solitary Norman. More than once I saw him staring over at us in puzzled fashion, but had no clue until, chancing to look at the Breton, I caught a glance of apprehension, almost of terror. Then Kerguelec murmured a low word, without significance for the others, even Rabaut paying it no heed.

"A sergeant—my father's regiment. When the revolution began, he helped murder the officers."

I understood it all in a flash—this devil of a Norman knew the de Rohan face, had either recognized Kerguelec or would do so shortly. The

146

results stood out too clearly. The fellow would make a denunciation before all of us, and to save his own position in the eyes of Fromond, Rabaut would not dare overlook it. To ascertain whether the supposed Kerguelec were really a woman would be only the work of a moment—

Sweat started on my face. Rabaut perceived it and made some jest about the heat of the day, but I caught a glance of comprehension from the dark, steady eyes of Kerguelec. With this I rose and went over to the table of the scowling captain.

Calling for some cold cider from the cellar, I began to talk with him about himself and his work here. Distracted from his suspicions, flattered by such attention from the assistant commissioner, he showed himself a most rabid republican. He did not hesitate even to go into certain details of countryside butchery.

I thought he was safe, but in the midst, as he flung a glance at Kerguelec, the half-frown vanished and his blue eyes flew suddenly wide. Recognition had come to him—I knew it without a word. He placed both hands on the table and started to jump up, when I leaned over and checked him.

"Wait, citizen!" I said quietly, not to draw the general attention. "I know it already."

These words broke into his sluggish mind. Staring at me, he sank back into his seat, and I went on with a confidence I was far from feeling.

"Yes, I know all about it! Finish your meal, then come outside with me, and we'll discuss the matter. It's an affair touching the republic itself, you comprehend?"

"Eh?" he blurted. "You mean—the disguised émigré yonder?"

By good fortune, the words passed unheard by our party. I nodded calmly.

"Of course. Citizen Rabaut knows it also. Do as I say, citizen captain, and I'll explain outside."

He obeyed, in his slow and ponderous fashion. For once, I was wholly at a loss. The fool must be silenced at any price—yet, Rabaut must not learn that I was aware of Kerguelec's identity. This put any appeal to Rabaut clear out of the question. How to clap a stopper on this rascal? The best solution would be to pistol him, but I was not minded to save Kerguelec at the immediate cost of my own head, especially after my warning had been spurned.

The captain finished his cider and rose. I followed and Rabaut glanced up.

PERIL FROM THE PAST IS SHARPEST

"We're starting at once, Martin! The tide is about full ebb."

I decided on a bold course—almost a desperate course. The dragoon was heading for the courtyard, so I beckoned Rabaut imperatively. He rose and came to me.

"Well?"

"This one," and I jerked my head toward the retiring captain, speaking in English, "has recognized in our friend Kerguelec some émigré in disguise."

Rabaut's arrogant eyes narrowed in swiftly startled dismay. I instantly took the advantage. It was obvious he did not want to lose Kerguelec's company.

"Now, émigré or not, I owe the Breton a debt," I went on easily. "You daren't turn over your hand, for Fromond is watching you like a cat."

"I know it, damnation take him!" muttered Rabaut.

"Well, leave the whole matter to me," I said confidently, now sure of him. "Don't warn Kerguelec —I'll handle the thing myself."

"Good," said Rabaut, only too glad to leave the onus of it on my shoulders.

I made haste outside, where the worthy captain

was lighting his pipe. He looked at me inquiringly.

"Well, citizen commissioner? Do you know this rascally Breton of yours is a woman—one of the accursed Rohans?"

"Certainly," I said. "And do you know that Cathelineau with an army of Whites is within a few miles of here?"

The officer looked at me, and the pipe fell from his hand to shatter on the stones of the courtyard.

"Cathelineau—here!" he said in a strangled voice. "Impossible!"

"Yet true," I assured him. "We nearly fell into his hands near Avranches, and this Breton saved us all. Citizen Rabaut is therefore in his, or her, debt. If someone else denounces her, he is clear of it—you understand? We must get on to the Mont at once, for Cathelineau may descend on this town any moment; he has destroyed detachments of our troops almost within sight of Avranches."

My rascal turned pale. "And my brave men, my little handful?"

"Must take their chance. Here! Let me solve the problem for you!"

He stammered something as he stared at me, his slow wits in a daze.

"Tell your dragoons to mount and ride for Avranches. You remain here. Ask this Breton to remain with you. Let Citizen Rabaut start for the Mont. I'll stay here, and we'll follow him ten minutes later. On the way, you will seize the Breton and take him in as your prisoner. Regard! You gain the shelter of the Mont, with a ci-devant in your hands, your men are saved, all is well— promotion and safety! Vive la République!"

He got my drift quickly enough, and if there were any holes in my argument the dreaded name of Cathelineau was a stopgap.

Two of his dragoons were lounging by the inn gate, and my officer strode hastily toward them. The effect of his words was immediate. They saluted and then made all haste to depart, shouting to their comrades down the street. At the same moment, Rabaut appeared, with Fromond and Ker-gueleç and the jeweler, calling our men from their dinner. The horses were brought out at once.

Here the Norman showed unexpected intelligence —perhaps a result of his spurring fear. He came up to the party and curtly desired Kerguelec to stop behind a few moments and give him some road information he could not obtain locally. Rabaut caught my nod, as did Kerguelec, and smoothed over the request in a casual manner. Rabaut, obviously, was very desirous not to draw Fromond into the matter.

"Very well," he assented. "Citizen Martin, will you wait with Kerguelec and bring along a bottle or two of this Calvados? Excellent stuff, this apple brandy, and if our Bastille yonder is damp as it looks, we'll be glad of a drop. Follow us soon."

"At once, citizen," I replied. The captain had gone off in search of his horse.

Rabaut called up our men, gave me one significant shrug, and rode away, Fromond and the jeweler with him. Fromond was far too impatient to reach the Mont for any passing suspicion or incident to find rest in his whirring head. So they rode away down the street toward the sands. Kerguelec came, bringing his horse and mine.

"Well?" he demanded briefly.

"For the last time, will you take the chance to escape or not?" I said angrily.

"For the last time, no!"

"Then ask no questions. Devil take me if I know what we'll do! Mount and ride."

We swung into the saddle, just as the captain appeared with his horse. He turned in on the other side of Kerguelec and we rode down the street. As we came from the village to the shining stretches of sand below the high dunes, the others were a quarter-mile ahead of us and striking off toward the Mont.

The dragoon was nervous, considerably perplexed in mind, and cursed the Whites most heartily for a pack of cowards who fought from behind hedges and were afraid to come into the open. Their style of combat was not to his taste, was not soldiering as he knew it. To do him justice, he was brave enough, though unnerved by thought of an invisible enemy, a bullet from the blue, and a firing-squad if captured.

We turned the final corner of the cliff, and out ahead of us appeared Mont St. Michael, the lower rock of Tombelaine beyond it. The Norman fell to cursing the place and threw out a hand at the sands.

"Six men went down there last week," he said. "Honest troopers, too—a fine day like this!"

"Went down?" I repeated. "How?"

"This accursed place of devils—if I were superstitious enough to think devils could exist! Quicksands are everywhere. Fog may come without a moment's notice. Sometimes the tide rushes in like a foaming wave, other times it simply appears— a man cannot run from it, even! Those six men were caught in fog and rising tide. It was the end of them."

I gave small credit to his words. The day was clear, hot, without trace of fog, and all these reports of swift tides struck me as wild folly. Here was no narrow bore, only huge level golden sands, league after league of them beyond eyesight. Quicksands, perhaps; yet from what I knew of such things, a man need merely keep his head to get clear, even if caught.

My thoughts were far more occupied with the question of my Norman captain. While entirely willing to kill him—there was no other possible course—it could scarcely be done out here on the open sands, in full sight of the whole shore, the Mont, the party ahead. In such case, Rabaut would be forced to arrest and hold me for some sort of trial, and I did not care to get into a dungeon at present. I had a vague idea of putting the man under arrest and having him flung into a cell on a trumped-up charge; yet this would be a desperate, implausible and futile effort. At least I had got rid of his dragoons, so that if my Norman did not return to Pontorson, he would not be readily missed.

We plodded on through the sand. Now I estimated it must be four miles to the Mont, rising ahead

PERIL FROM THE PAST IS SHARPEST

of us majestic and isolated, all gray naked stone from this aspect. Details of the place grew upon us. The shore was girded abruptly with ramparts, save where cliff shot up in sheer straight masses.

Slightly to the left was a massive tower and cluster of buildings, marking the entrance-gate of the place. From this, in an ascending transverse line toward the right, appeared other buildings, former inns and taverns for pilgrims. Those were backed by the naked rock, sweeping up in almost incredible lines of masonry to the spiring abbey that topped the whole. The closer we drew, the more upon us all grew the wonder of this ancient structure.

"One can understand," murmured Kerguelec, "why this abbey was always called simply 'The Marvel'! It seems a place made by angels—"

As though these words had wakened him, the dragoon turned in his saddle, drew out a pistol, and fastened his blue eyes on Kerguelec.

"You're under arrest, ci-devant," he announced brusquely. "You are no man, but a woman. I know your face—one of those damned aristocrats calling themselves de Rohans! Well, there is no longer a 'de' in France, you comprehend? I know you."

SAINT MICHAEL'S GOLD

"So you should," said Kerguelec, meeting his look with calm gaze. "Since you served in my father's regiment—traitor to your salt and your king!"

"Hand over your pistols, Kerguelec," I demanded roughly. Between this insolence and that contempt, a spark of death might well fly. "Hand them over, and no more talk. You're a prisoner."

We were now perhaps two miles from the Mont, and a like distance from the shore, as we did not hit out directly for the place but at a sharp angle from Pontorson. The 'party ahead had gained somewhat upon us. Kerguelec, without protest, took the two pistols from his sash and handed them to me. The dragoon watched frowningly.

"Are the loads fresh?" I asked.

"Yes."

I looked to the priming, and then, thrusting away one pistol, cocked the other. The crisis had come—there was nothing for it now but action. And yet, in this moment, I could not deliberately and without a word shoot down the man; it went against the grain, savored too much of murder outright, was in fact nothing else.

I glanced up from the pistol and was about to speak and give him at least a chance, when I saw

156

he was staring with uplifted eyes at the horizon. A low exclamation of surprise broke from him.

"Name of the dead devil! Something is happening!"

Something was indeed happening—though, as I followed his gaze, I could not for a moment place it. Then I realized the sunlight was thinning out, imperceptibly and strangely, for not a cloud broke the blue sky. This very blue, too, seemed to be fading and losing its hot color. Kerguelec spoke in a queer voice.

"Tombelaine—look!"

The island beyond the Mont, a huge bit of rock not unlike a crouching lion, slowly vanished from before our sight and was gone, even as we looked. With this I had the explanation and laughed a little.

"Mist," I said. "Mist in the distance. Well, citizen captain, you know this Breton to be a ci-devant and a woman, do you? A returned émigré, eh?"

The dragoon remembered himself again, forgot the mist. He jerked his head around and looked steadily at me.

"Yes," he said at last. "Of course."

"But when she is denounced, she will certainly

be imprisoned, and very likely executed. Do you realize the fact?"

"I hope so." He flung a brutally savage look at Kerguelec. "If I had my way, every one of them would be shot on sight without a trial, men and women and children—the whole accursed breed must be wiped out!"

"Yes!" I said calmly. "But, citizen captain, you mistake about this one."

He gave me a blank, uncomprehending stare.

"How, a mistake? Not a bit of it, citizen. Search for yourself, you'll see she's a woman— bah! What need of search! Lily-smooth hands and neck, no touch of a beard, a bit full in the breast and hips, eh? Besides, you heard what she said, admitting her identity. When I denounce her—"

"You'll not denounce her, you street-sweepings," I said, and flung up my cocked pistol at him. "Drop those weapons—quick!"

At this instant, absolutely without any warning, the dragoon was literally blotted from my sight. In the twinkling of an eye a thick blanket of fog enveloped us.

CHAPTER VIII

IT IS EASY TO MAKE PLANS

I THINK the incredible celerity of this thick mist held all three of us paralyzed for an instant, despite the crisis upon us, and drew our startled attention from each other to the misty vapor around. We had seen no bank of fog moving forward; it had apparently sprung full-bodied from the ground, thick and white as powder-smoke. The figure of Kerguelec, at arm's length from me, was a dim shape. That of the captain had vanished.

Abruptly, Kerguelec caught my arm, dragging me over in the saddle and almost unseating me. The red flash of a pistol split the fog, and the bullet sang close. I straightened up and fired a response, but already the horses had broken into a plunging gallop and I nearly went to the sand.

I recovered my reins, dropped the pistol, and got my horse under control. Looking around, I found myself alone. The others had completely disappeared in this accursed fog.

159

SAINT MICHAEL'S GOLD

"Kerguelec!"

No reply to my shout, and my voice was beat back and muffled by the dense, smooth whiteness. Whither the brief dash had carried me, was problematical, and all sense of direction was totally lost. Still, we could not be far from the spreading waters of the Couesnon River, losing themselves somewhere in the sands close by, and thus, by finding the trickle, might at least have a guide back to the coast—unless a quicksand intervened. Indeed, with the captain escaped, we might have to make for the coast and give up any further idea of going to the Mont—flee south, instead, into the Vendée!

I slipped from the saddle. For a long moment I knelt, applying my ear to the sand, listening. I caught a dull sound, and again; listened more intently—and then glanced up to find my horse gone from sight. The thickness of the mist was incredible. I leaped up, went dashing into the fog only to encounter nothing, and halted with an imprecation on my own folly. Now I was dismounted as well as lost.

Since remaining in one spot would certainly be of no avail, I struck out at random, one pistol ready, hoping at least to run across my horse again. Well for me I was thus prepared! For a time nothing

IT IS EASY TO MAKE PLANS

happened. Perhaps ten minutes in all passed. I shouted repeatedly, but no reply came, and I knew a mere voice could not hope to pierce the fog for any great distance.

I was on the point of firing in the air as a signal, when to one side of me loomed a dark mass, indistinct, formless. Instantly came the burst of a shot, and the bullet whipped through my riding cloak.

The pistol in my hand made response, and I was sure of a hit. Yet, when I leaped forward, horse and rider had disappeared completely, and I gripped at the empty air. It was uncanny, disconcerting, baffling in the extreme. I dropped the second pistol, having my own brace still remaining, and shouted.

Immediately upon this there came to me from one side the repeated hooting of a screech-owl, and I hastily turned toward it. Kerguelec must have heard the shots and was signaling to me; the cry was used by the peasant royalists as a signal— whence the term of Chouan applied to their leader and to them in Maine.

So I plunged ahead more confidently, only to come to a confused halt on finding the signal grow-ing fainter and farther. The fog was deceiving me. I called again, and now we began a pretty game of blindman's buff, against the chance of the Norman captain lighting upon either of us. Hoot and shout were repeated time and again— until of a sudden burst forth a new and terrible voice. It was the thin scream of a horse, instinct with awful fear and terror, flinging across the fog a note of shrill, soul-shaken panic. It came again and again, ever more fraught with panic, and served to guide me. Then close by Kerguelec cried out to me—this time in a scream, the desperate scream of a woman, all her caution lost in sudden frantic horror.

No mistake about it now, the sound came just from my right, and I ran toward it blindly, cocking a pistol as I ran. Without warning my feet seemed to go down into fluid sand, and even as I realized the peril, I could discern close ahead of me a struggling mass, almost within touching distance before it became visible.

No need for weapon here! I was upon them abruptly, thrust away the pistol, caught in my arms a dim figure leaping toward me—Kerguelec.

"Quick, quick! The horse!"

I saw the poor brute was already in far over fetlocks, almost to knees, straining terribly yet caught beyond escape. No help for it. Another frightful scream whirred up, then I pulled out the pistol and mercifully put a bullet into the head of the trapped animal. I myself was down to the ankles by this time, yet managed to pull clear easily enough, since Kerguelec had me by the hand.

"Out of here, now!" I exclaimed. Even in this moment I noticed the slim delicacy of the fingers gripping to mine. "Keep your head, step rapidly —hold together!"

"Your horse—"

"Lost. The dragoon, too, worse luck! We may have to hit for the shore—"

Upon this began for the two of us a veritable dance of death, since it proved we were close to the little river, where the moving, sucking sands were dangerous in the extreme. Here and there we came upon brooks of water in the sand, yet dared not try to get across them, for there lay peril. Withal we must keep moving, always moving. At each instant we might plunge down, and I had quite lost all my contempt for these quicksands in acute conscious-ness of their deadliness.

Time passed. In whatever direction we turned, we appeared to find only the same loose danger, until at length a gasp of relief broke from Kerguelec and we plunged forward to a stretch of firm sand. We halted, and if Kerguelec was trembling, I was streaming with cold sweat. For a space we rested in silence, gained poise and breath.

"The tide will be coming in soon," I said. "It looks as though the Norman had escaped, and so we'd better give up the Mont and make for the coast. The trickle of water and the ripples in the sand will guide us."

"No!" exclaimed Kerguelec firmly. "I go on to the Mont—it is imperative."

An angry response was on my lips, when it was checked by something dark, ahead, dimly visible through the cloaking vapor. Almost stepping on it before I realized, I found myself looking down at the body of the dragoon captain. He lay still clutching a pistol—my last bullet must have reached him, for he was shot through the heart, quite dead. Kerguelec drew me on with a shiver and asked no questions. Then abruptly the Breton clutched my hand tightly, halted, glanced around.

"Listen! There is someone behind us—I heard it——"

Almost at our heels sounded with startling clarity a long-drawn sigh, and then another, as though of one in pain. Perhaps we were both unnerved by the situation, and the memory of the dead man lying

IT IS EASY TO MAKE PLANS

somewhere in the sand behind us lingered heavily. Upon me fell a nameless horrible apprehension—the fear coming from an invisible presence in a dark room. I called out sharply.

"Who's there? Speak——"

Silence answered. We started forward and a sighing gasp reached us again so that a low cry burst from Kerguelec. Hand in hand we plunged on a few steps until I stopped and uttered a shaky laugh of relief, half angry at myself for such folly.

"Nothing but the air in the wet sand, comrade—listen!"

To my footstep, came the sigh. Kerguelec laughed, but ended the laugh sharply.

"It means that the tide is coming in then—the water is seeping up through the sand! Run for it——"

"Keep cool," I counselled, and leaned over to seek direction from the ripples in the sand. As I did so, distinct along the surface I caught the rolling, rattling reverberation of drums.

"They're sounding drums at the Mont. We're close by! Wait, now, and listen——"

We both heard it clearly, when putting ear to sand, though when erect the sound was quite inaudible to us. Rabaut had obviously reached the

165

island and was attempting to guide us in, realizing our peril. It now became a question of orientation, since we were on firm sand once again. Careful inspection of the sand under our feet showed the direction of the water-ripples and we started off at a good pace, pausing now and again to listen for the drums.

"We're making it aright," I said in no little relief. "And that rascally Norman won't bother you further."

"But his men!" Kerguelec turned a white, anxious face to me. "When he does not return they'll send——"

"They'll never know." Laughing, I explained by what stratagem I had got rid of the dragoons. "Your greatest danger will lie from Rabaut, comrade. Do you know he is planning to get away with the treasure to America?"

"By your help?"

I read the thought behind the words, and chuckled. "So he thinks. No, no, I don't want your monastic gold! If we get away with it, you'll be welcome to the lot, for your cause or king or——"

"Pardon, my friend." Kerguelec pressed my hand. "I did not mean such——"

The Breton's voice died, and we both came to a

IT IS EASY TO MAKE PLANS

halt. A ragged volley of musketry broke through the fog thinly, but it was not this bringing us to pause. Every thought was swept away in a cold access of fear—around our feet was water, where an instant before had been sand. The tide was coming in!

"To the left," I said. "Run!"

Even on the words we were ankle-deep. Panic seized us. Hand in hand we broke into a run once more, and sharp peril spurred us. We splashed ahead, floundered on through fast-deepening swirls of water, at our knees before we knew it. The rapidity of this devilish tide was indeed something incredible, though it came in no wave. Kerguelec gave up the effort, came to a halt.

"Useless!" he groaned. "We're caught, comrade."

He jerked out the little wooden rosary and stood with head bowed over it. I caught at it, tore it away, then seized him by the shoulder and forced him on.

"Don't give up! We're close by the island——"

Close by, indeed! Echoing my words came another burst of shots, and then a puff of wind struck my cheek. The fog eddied and swirled in ghostly shapes, and thinned. I let out a shout and

Kerguelec repeated it. Directly ahead loomed up a mountainous shape, dark, indistinct. The water was nearly to our waists now climbing swiftly and surely.

"Fifty yards more—all's well!"

Shouts reached us, and more shots, to which I responded. Then I lost footing and went under, to come up swimming and laughing.

"Swim, Breton!"

With a gasp of relief he gave up the struggle to keep erect—both of us were well nigh exhausted. A poor swimmer, he could just manage to keep going. Meantime more wind, and over us the fog thinned and dissipated, while men came splashing out from shore with lines. Next moment they were around us, swimming, wading, hauling us in. We had landed at the very gate of the Mont. And as we staggered in from the water across the little space of firm ground, the fog became all shot with pallid sunlight and then was gone on the wings of brilliant afternoon, as though in despair of catching more victims for this time.

About us crowded soldiers and half a dozen Montois, as the local inhabitants were termed—rough, gnarled fishermen whose jargon was nearly unintelligible. Oaths, exclamations, shouts, filled the air. Through them came shoving Rabaut, more human feeling in his face than I had ever thought to see.

"Good!" he cried out, giving a hand to each of us, but all his eyes to Kerguelec. "You had a near thing of it—eh? Soaked! Here, a swallow of cognac——"

A gulp of the fiery stuff, then he brought us into the guardroom above the courtyard, just inside the main gate. He curtly excluded all others, while we dropped on a bench to recover, then he turned with a keen glance at me.

"Well, Martin? Where's the dragoon officer?"

"Ask the tide and the quicksands," I returned. "Kerguelec's horse went down—had to shoot the poor brute—and I lost mine. We nearly went down likewise. Brr! Fromond knew what he was talking about when he warned us from those sands!"

Rabaut nodded, and his face cleared at my news.

"Aye," he assented. "According to the people here, neither the tide, the fog nor the sands are dangerous—taken separately; but together they're murderous. Well, we all have a long climb ahead to our quarters—if you're able, we'd better be going. I've ordered clothes and rooms made ready, but have not been up to the abbey yet. We can't get to work until to-morrow. That devil Fromond is raging about it! I nearly had to arrest him. All ready? Then we'll be off."

We were all right in no time, and followed Rabaut out to the street. A shout of delight from the soldiers and hearty congratulations greeted us, but I noticed that the handful of Montois now held aloof in sullen, scowling silence. The reason for this attitude was not long in appearing. Rabaut, who knew the place well from other days, needed no guide and led us forward himself.

Directly ahead, a tremendous mass of masonry linked the outer ramparts to the cliff on our left; this mass was pierced by a large closed gate and an open postern through which we entered—this was the King's Tower and gate, an inner defence. Now before us opened up the single street mounting, in a saber-like curve, to the battlements and abbey above.

On either hand the street was lined with a solid row of taverns and shops, where in former days the flocks of pilgrims had been entertained and loaded down with relics and souvenirs of all sorts; as late as the previous summer pilgrims had come here. Now all the place was closed, empty, desolate,

IT IS EASY TO MAKE PLANS

for the Mont Libre knew no more pilgrims. One inn alone was open, the Red Unicorn. Deprived of their sole livelihood, the Montois had either scattered to other places or remained as apathetic fishermen, ruined by the revolution and not at all appreciating the bliss of freedom.

The way was steep and sharply cobbled where it did not traverse the naked rock. To spare Kerguelec, I called a halt at the next turn and got my pipe alight with some half-soaked tobacco from my pouch. From Rabaut's remarks, as he took snuff and gazed around, I concluded he must have had some intimate acquaintance with this royal prison in former times—perhaps from the wrong side of the walls. Certainly he seemed to hold the abbey in a species of dormant hatred.

Farther on appeared long curving stairways and terraces, all of stone, endlessly mounting in a high vista across the shoulder of the peak, and there doubling back out of sight. Upon me grew a clearer perception of how enormous this whole place was in extent, and what untold labor had built it. When we paused again, Rabaut pointed to a cobbled wall and a pile of ruins, to our left.

"Bertrand du Guesclin built that house for his bride," he said, and added cynically: "And what would Edward the Confessor have thought, when he climbed this hill had he foreseen we should one day walk in his steps?"

"Probably," said Kerguelec, with the first open speech I had heard him direct at Rabaut, "he would have extirpated the family of St.-Servaut."

This shot, and the allusion to his ancient stock, did not please Citizen Rabaut. He gave the Breton a sidelong glance and then smiled in his mirthless grimace.

"Yes!" he said softly. "But once allied to the house of de Rohan, what would St.-Servaut have to fear from kings?"

Kerguelec did not respond. Rabaut thought the meaning of these words lost upon me, but they showed me his intent; and I could see the Breton's silence came from face-white anger. Marriage offered any de Rohan by such a man, or compelled, was the worst of outrages. So at least thought Kerguelec in bitter pride of race, but I smiled to myself—there were far worse matters in the world, as he might yet discover.

We went on in silence after this, until at length we paused again on a wide terrace near the crumbling ramparts, where they curved up to meet the abbey walls. It was necessary to toil up this

IT IS EASY TO MAKE PLANS

long sloping succession of stairs to attain even a vague comprehension of what the abbey yet far above us meant in the way of ancient labor and skill. It towered there incredibly, a cluster of buildings rearing into the sky, a gloomily threatening mass of stone. All this granite had been fetched hither from the Chausey Islands to the west, one of the abbey fiefs in former days. Few soldiers were visible, and I inquired as to the reason.

"Few are here," and Rabaut shrugged. "A handful could hold the place against an army, but who would attack? No wandering band of Whites could hope to take the Mont, and it is not worth sending an army against—we could too easily throw in reenforcements from Avranches or by water. The place has no military value these days. The local militia and a few invalided regulars are here— no more; they have more need to tend the cooking fires than their muskets. Three hundred priests are locked up yonder, like sheep to guard, for all are infirm or aged. No, little use here for soldiers."

Thought of the living conditions under which those three hundred captives must labor brought a chill.

We passed on from landing to landing, then

toiled up a final sharp flight of stairs against a wall, and so came to the Chatelet—a tiny black opening between two enormous towers. Inside were more steps; the entire approach was built for defence, and a glance showed it to be absolutely impregnable. Indeed, as Rabaut said, the place had stood more than one siege, yet had never been captured or reduced by an enemy.

Sentinels saluted, and a soldier joined us as guide with a bunch of huge keys. Inside the Chatelet, we climbed on to a wide platform beneath the gate-towers. Off to our right appeared a guardroom and a deep courtyard, but our way lay straight ahead under the blue sky, yet into a stupendous cañon of stone. Still it wound steeply upward, passed from landing to stairs again, and now all between towering gray masonry. On the left hand were the abbatial buildings, and on the right the huge masses of the church foundations. The basilica proper was far overhead, being the crown of the whole work, and looking upward it seemed as though we had not yet begun our ascent. The realization was stupefying.

A hundred feet up this steep road, known as the Great Inner Degree, our guide turned to a doorway on the left, entering the abbatial buildings. Here, he

174

informed us, were rooms in some sort made ready for occupancy, although the entire place was in mad confusion.

We passed into the building and followed up endless flights of narrow stone stairs. The structure was empty, untenanted, given over these three years to neglect and desolation. After a time we came to a great room hung with tattered tapestries, its once splendid furnishings hacked and its paintings ripped. Rabaut turned to Kerguelec, after conferring with the guide.

"You had best keep this room. He tells me there is no lack of monkish apparel in these wardrobes, so you can get into dry garments."

Kerguelec assented in silence. I passed on with Rabaut to another tremendous chamber, also bearing clear signs of devastation. Here our guide went his way. Rabaut drew me to a window opening on the Great Inner Degree and pointed to a carven stone gallery or bridge flung across the top of this great chasm of masonry, leading to the church.

"You see the advantages of our situation, Martin? The treasure is kept over yonder, and this bridge gives us quick and easy access to all the upper portion of the place——"

175

SAINT MICHAEL'S GOLD

"At the present moment," I broke in, "my chief interest lies in dry clothes."

Rabaut laughed. "True! Well, I've none to offer, but my services are at your command. Here's food and wine waiting; we'll dine in the refectory to-night, and perhaps this wardrobe will afford something——"

He smashed open a huge oak Norman wardrobe half filling one wall, and triumphantly drew forth an armful of cassocks, monkish robes and other paraphernalia, which he flung at me gaily. I stripped, clad myself warmly if not becomingly in approved Benedictine costume, and sat down to the table to split a bottle of wine with him.

Rabaut was in expansive mood, but I had no illusions whatever about his confidence in me. He thought me a trusting dupe, and without doubt meant to murder or get rid of me the moment he had the treasure safe and was in no more need of my help. Since discovering the secret of Kerguelec, the man had imperceptibly but surely altered toward me, and I was too much on the alert not to sense a certain duplicity in his manner.

"Why not go openly to America as an agent of the republic?" he asked, his eyes kindling to the idea. "My commission gives me full powers, and

176

papers are easily forged. After a month, say, when the gold is safely converted and banked, I can sever my connection with diplomacy and drop out of sight."

"All very well," I returned, "but what if an English frigate overhauls our lugger en route to America?"

His face became a mask. "I've prepared for all contingencies," he said. "The lugger will be off Tombelaine in three days. I shall requisition a fishing boat here—there are only half a dozen—and it will await my orders. When we leave, I replace the local guards with those Alsatians we brought. You and I and the two Parisians, Pol Rouge and Pol Noir, will load the gold in the boat and depart. It's very simple."

"Very," I echoed drily. These words showed already he intended to get rid of me before departing. Probably he would do it at the last moment. He made no mention of Kerguelec, and his avoidance was significant. He did however put a negligent question designed to test me out a trifle.

"By the way, Martin, did that dragoon officer say for whom he took our Breton? Some noble, perhaps?"

"He mentioned the name of de Rohan," I replied,

with equal indifference, "but had no time to elaborate on the theme. He was careless with his pistols."

Rabaut showed white teeth in his mirthless grin and was satisfied. A fine demagogue this heartless scoundrel, traitor to everything and everyone except what he deemed his own self-interest!

"Where's Fromond?" I asked.

"Looting the library, I believe." Rabaut shook his head frowningly. "There's madness in that fellow! Well, do you care to have a look around? I'd like to look over the place once again from a standpoint of authority. We might go——"

"Like this?" I asked with a grimace at my black-clad figure.

"Why not? Here's a pair of sandals to go with the costume," and he kicked a pair of mildewed sandals across the floor.

What matter, after all? I donned the sandals, lighted my pipe, and rose.

We did not go down to the bottom of the Inner Degree, that gulf between gray walls slowly winding upward, but by way of the abbatial passage—the bridge crossing from the abbot's rooms directly to the church, and opening into the chapel of the Trinity. Here we found a soldier enthusiastically

IT IS EASY TO MAKE PLANS

painting republican mottoes and chipping away carvings, and we pressed him into service as cicerone, for Rabaut knew little of the abbey. His acquaintance, I conjectured, had been chiefly with the prisons.

We found ourselves in a church whose quiet splendor rose magnificently above crass destruction, and for once Rabaut even was awed. No hands had reached these high vaulted arches, whose delicacy of carving was calculated to make the place seem yet larger than it was in reality; yet it was only a mere shell of former grandeur. Plain bare walls were left of the ambulatory and its seven chapels. The altars had been ruthlessly splintered and smashed, the carven figures all hacked to fragments.

Choir and sanctuary, lifting in Gothic elegance to the high windows, remained only as vestiges of past beauty. The stone floor was strewn with bits of ancient stained glass, the sculptured and carven stalls had been smashed; all around lay bits of statuary and savagely ripped paintings. Along the walls a few bas-reliefs had somehow escaped the general devastation and testified to the former glory of the whole. The high altar of St. Michael, between choir and nave, had long since been stripped of its silver covering and was no more than a ruinous mass of wood and stone.

From the church our guide conducted us to the cloister, a covered gallery around a large central opening. Rabaut touched me on the arm and spoke in a low voice.

"This is said to be the most beautiful piece of architecture in all France. Imagine such a place subject to the spiteful hatred of our Citizen Fromond!"

I could understand his feeling, little as he himself loved the Mont. The double row of small, delicate columns supporting the vaulted gallery were of pink granite, surmounted by the most intricate carvings in white stone. The walls, spaced with blind arcades and stone seats, held exquisite bas-reliefs and carvings, now mutilated. The perfect proportion, the balanced beauty of the whole, was something beyond credence.

Our guide fell into a blasphemous and chuckling recital of how, something over a year earlier, bands from the towns along the coast had descended upon the Mont, sweeping through it with wild destruction, burning the charter-house and wrecking everything until the militia from Avranches halted the work. Rabaut silenced him with an abrupt, angry

IT IS EASY TO MAKE PLANS

word. This place had made an impression upon Citizen Rabaut, so much so that he drew a long breath of relief when we came out upon the west platform fronting the main doors of the church.

Here in the open air everything seemed different, fresher, the dazzling summer afternoon sunlight bathing everything in a golden glow of sharp reality. From this tremendous platform was ordinarily a view of Mount Dol and beyond, over Brittany to the south and Normandy to the north, but now the fog still cloaked down over sea and land. Above the waves of white cloud, the Mont hung as though suspended in the sunlit heavens, out of the world.

Still we had the revolution with us. Midway of the great platform was affixed a pike, crowned with a red liberty cap—a center for dancing and the new worship no doubt. Beyond this, near the verge of the platform, was set up a table at which sat our Citizen Fromond. The jeweler and two of the Alsatian soldiers were heaping armfuls of rolls and manuscripts on the table and stones around—contents of the once famed library, such as remained after the looting of the previous year. Fromond, it appeared, was packing up the volumes to carry back to Avranches, not from any love of learning but from a desire to root out everything of value belonging to the monks.

As we looked on, one of the soldiers opened up a folio of vellum and tore out a magnificent page illumined in gold and colors—a jolly little gift for his chidren, he said with a grin. Fromond cursed him sullenly but offered no objection and gave us a dark look. Rabaut shrugged and turned away.

Along the edge of the platform had once run a stone parapet, now shattered and gone. We advanced to it, and Rabaut held out his hand in silent gesture to the sheer gulf below, ending in water and black rock. I questioned him and learned the captive priests were in the dungeons below, as well as in the old hostelry of the abbey, now half in ruins.

"One or two of the poor fools tried to escape some days ago," and Rabaut laughed thinly. "It would matter little if any of them walked away; however, they found some rope and tried an evasion."

"And they accomplished it?" I asked.

"They saved all hands a lot of trouble." Rabaut took a pinch of snuff with his elegant air and gestured to the gulf. "The ropes broke."

I shivered slightly. "If I were Cathelineau, I'd raid this place some night, for the sake of the treasure and the priests."

IT IS EASY TO MAKE PLANS

"Impossible, without an army. The blackbirds are too infirm to get away," said Rabaut. A few months later, indeed, the truth of his words was proven. "Besides, they could not reach here without conquering the whole country as they went. Ah, well! In the morning we start working our gold-mine. Shall we have a look at the rest of the place, Citizen Martin?"

I assented with a nod, glad to get away from here. The bitter, twisted face of Fromond haunted me.

CHAPTER IX

NEXT morning brought me from slumber to dazzling sunlight, pouring into my south-looking chamber. Lying in the once stately bed, whose posts and tester were broken and ripped, I thought again dreamily of the previous evening and its unrealities—of our ill-cooked dinner in the huge refectory with its smashed windows, its high carvings and reader's lectern, its ghosts of knightly days; of Kerguelec, in stained and wrinkled Breton garb, of Rabaut's cynicism, of the wondrous hall of the Chevaliers, the floor littered with torn banners of the knights of St. Michael. And now I wakened to a frowzy soldier bringing me bread and wine, with word that Citizens Fromond and Rabaut were at work. He had no need to specify the nature of the work. He advised me to drink no water, since all in the place was bad, and departed.

Having dressed and breakfasted, I visited Ker-

184

THE PAST CAUSES THE PRESENT

guelec's room next to mine and found him gone. I went on to the church, crossing the Inner Degree by the bridge, and in the basilica met two of our Alsatian troopers. Each was hauling across the floor, by a rope, a large fish-tub filled to the brim with all manner of gold and silver objects, from chalices to crucifixes. In reply to my queries, they pointed to the open west doors of the church. I preceded them and came out upon the same great platform where we had seen Fromond the previous afternoon. To all appearance, he had been there ever since.

It was a most curious scene that greeted me—the more so because I could comprehend the underlying significance of each detail. Rabaut, knowing this, regarded me with his cynical half-smile.

He sat at the table, set for sake of the cool breeze close to the dizzy edge of the platform. At the opposite side of the table sat Fromond; between them was the crafty-eyed jeweler with his scales set up and at work. I advanced to the side of Rabaut, whence I could look down directly into the gulf below. One glance at it was quite enough for me, and I gave my attention to the work in hand.

Before Rabaut lay the inventory of abbey property, made out by the last prior, Dom François Maurice—who had, I understood, sympathized with

185

the revolution in its early stages. The document was dated April 10, 1790. As each object was weighed and appraised, Rabaut checked it off on the inventory, while Fromond made notes of the price offered by the jeweler. Our four Alsatians were bringing up the treasure, some objects separately, others loaded into fish-tubs. The things all ready and checked were being separated, some being wrapped, others stuffed into stout leathern bags for transport —these, the more valuable. Rabaut, cynically open, was coolly directing them with a look or word in this separation, and I guessed the leathern bags were intended for his own ultimate transport.

What a treasure it was! The sight of it was stupendous. More startling was the realization of its artistic and historic value, as I glanced from the glittering heaps to the inventory lying on the table. Each object, and its provenance, was fully described there. As I looked on, the jeweler weighed and appraised at five thousand francs the great pastoral cross of silver, noted as having been made in 1412 and as being the most beautiful in all France. He picked up an abbot's miter of the same period, heavily adorned with large pearls and precious stones, and estimated its value with a shrug of deprecation. I saw Rabaut quietly shake his head at the two

THE PAST CAUSES THE PRESENT

soldiers—the miter was too bulky. The irony of this plunder-picking under Fromond's eyes was amusing.

Around us stood tub after tub, some filled with general objects, others with reliquaries, others with the peculiar votive hearts offered by pilgrims at this shrine. Fascinated, I smoked and watched proceedings for an hour or more.

Splendid reliquaries were opened by Fromond, who tossed the contents out into the gulf with blazing jests. Ancient enamels were appraised at a song. Three silver gilt candelabra, given by the Duke of Bourbon in 1329, went at five hundred francs and were rejected by Rabaut, who would have only gold or gems. There was no lack of either. When the reliquaries were finished, the first object fished up from the next tub was a large gold chain and medallion presented by Louis XI in 1470. I began to comprehend the astonishing age and inviolability of this place, whose historic splendors were thus being checked off to the melting pot like so many peltries just arrived from a trading-post!

After a time, Rabaut signed me to take his place. For the moment, the gold was at ebb; a half-dozen tubs of silver and brass ornaments and ex-votos were next on the lists, and these did not interest the

187

worthy citizen commissioner. Rabaut took his departure, and the two Parisians saluted him solemnly. "Vive la République! Vive la nation!" they repeated in unison, uttering the fetish of the revolution like two automatons.

I regarded these two men, Pol Rouge and Pol Noir, unobtrusively but with growing interest. They revered Rabaut as the symbol and living authority of Paris, as indeed he was; at the session of May sixth, I had heard more than one member of the convention denounce the system of commissioners, as giving each man the power of a king, yet it was an efficient and excellent system in general. None could foretell who would be a Judas, and someone had to be trusted, so that to the common folk a commissioner was all of revolutionary France personified.

Yet I perceived these two grenadiers ignored me. More, their manner of doing it was heavy and labored; it amused me, but also gave food for thought. They were clumsy fellows, and I could see clearly how Rabaut had informed them against me—they had been picked to murder or put me out of the way when the right time came, and were already instructed in this duty. Indirect evidence, of course, still plain enough.

THE PAST CAUSES THE PRESENT

As the morning wore on to noon, my attention was turned to observing Fromond more than anyone else. At first he had been excited, eager, full of snarling blasphemous exultancies, as one who comes to a long-antipicated goal. Then he gradually became quiet. Upon him descended an air of absorbed fanaticism, yet it seemed to me that he was grimly pushing his way forward against invisible but terrible counter-force. The twisted left side of his face broke into occasional nervous twitching, his cruel and powerful lips wore a set snarl, and his air to the rest of us was singularly wild and bitter.

Odd as it might appear, the man was actually very self-conscious while sitting here at his work. He was posing again, to himself or to the devil within him. Aware of how I had previously pierced his apparent frenetic fury, no doubt recalling my extremely blunt words to him, he now and again darted glances across the table at me, as he brought up some object and handed it to the jeweler.

These looks were ominous and swift as summer lightning. On each occasion his pale blue eyes stabbed into me, venomous with hatred and fear. No words passed, yet it was easy to understand how tense was the man, how ready to burst forth at

189

any pretext. So I gave him none. The open enmity of Rabaut would have been far less disquieting to me than the silent, deadly, hidden antagonism of this strange individual. And all the while, behind the blaze of the blue eyes, lay a nameless and frightful horror, puzzling to observe—as though it were horror of himself and his actions.

Noon wore on, and by common consent we knocked off work. Far beneath us, all this time, had been going on the usual routine of the prison quarters and dungeons. I scarce realized this until a soldier came to announce the noonday meal ready in the refectory. Then a low sound of chanting voices drifted up to us, and with a suppressed oath Fromond inquired concerning it.

"Our black-robed guests, citizen procureur!" returned the soldier, and grinned. "They whine a superstitious psalm or two at times. It does no harm and amuses them——"

"Order them to be silent!" snapped Fromond. "Let the dogs do their whining at night, if they must do it!"

Even the soldier was astonished, for these local militia were not bad fellows in their way, being rather tolerant, and had none of the rabid savagery of our Alsatian troopers. He shrugged and re-

THE PAST CAUSES THE PRESENT

turned below, while we passed into the cloister and so toward the refectory. Here we came upon Rabaut and Kerguelec, who had been walking in the cool shade. The Breton gave me one peculiar, imperative look, but I wholly failed to read its significance.

Our meal was none too good. Besides, I think most of us were rather oppressed by the sense of desecration hanging about the place. The only one of us in high spirits was the Norman jeweler, who stood to make a small fortune from his bargain after he had melted down the precious metals and sold the others. Once or twice I caught Rabaut eyeing him speculatively and coldly, and so recalled how this crafty little man was a spy of the committee at Avranches, as well as a jeweler. Citizen Rabaut, I reflected, had one or two people to get rid of if he were to cover up his tracks effectively, and I wondered how he would go about it.

He did not intend to do it by making friends with Fromond, as became clear while we were still at table. A guard from below brought a petition from the captives there. Learning of the arrival of a commissioner, the aged priests begged they might have liberty to leave their prisons and walk in the garden or about the abbey, since the heat of summer was affecting them sorely and half of them were ill from the pestilential water of the Mont—most of it rainwater stored from the past winter.

Fromond interjected a scathing flood of abuse and commanded hotly that the priests remain where they were and be thankful. I saw Kerguelec touch Rabaut's arm, saw those steady dark eyes prick a message, and comprehended how the Breton must be playing to make trouble. Rabaut took a pinch of snuff, leaned back in his chair, and looked steadily at Fromond.

"Citizen procureur," he said loudly, deliberately and coldly, "there is something you have forgotten —something really of the highest importance, I assure you!"

"What?" snapped Fromond.

"The fact that you are not giving orders here, and I am." Rabaut flung a nod to the guard. "Very good. Let the old men wander about. They are harmless. They will not be allowed to leave these upper buildings for the town below, but they may have a breath of air. You have no complaint as to their conduct?"

"None, citizen commissaire," returned the soldier. "They are as children. The one who tried to escape

THE PAST CAUSES THE PRESENT

last week, and was dropped into the sea, was the only young one among them."

Rabaut dismissed him and gave Fromond a hard look. The lawyer, though white-faced with anger, refused the challenge and swallowed his wrath.

After the meal there was no indication of an immediate return to our labor, so I passed into the cool depths of the church, idly regarding the work of destruction and wondering whether this looting of an ancient fane were not to be the means of saving my own life and liberty. A footstep brought me about to see Kerguelec approaching with a gesture toward the huge, four-columned pillars close by. I joined him in shelter of one, and he addressed me with a brusque, almost peremptory air.

"What share of the treasure will you take to assist me?"

"None," I responded, trying to probe the meaning behind the words. "I want none of it and will not assist you to obtain it. To assist you in a personal manner—that's another thing. Which is it?"

Kerguelec smiled, and suddenly the woman flashed out in this smile, marvelously.

"If I cannot obtain it, then I must insure it does not reach Paris. The assistance is personal, to put it so, in this endeavor."

193

SAINT MICHAEL'S GOLD

"Then why insult me with the offer of gold?"

"To see if the sight of it has affected you," was the dry response. "Evidently it has not done so. You are the man you look, and I apologize. Your assistance?"

"Granted, as you might know," I said promptly. "The best of the treasure won't reach Paris in any case, if I know it. What's happened that you appeal for help?"

"Rabaut," came the significant rejoinder. "I've discovered that I am playing a rather risky game——"

"Oh! Wonderful discovery!" I laughed ironically. "You who refuse warnings——"

"Will not refuse help." The words carried much in their tone of almost despondent realization, and I scrutinized the smooth, delicate features of Kerguelec with some care. It seemed to me he had been badly shaken.

"You must have had a very pleasant talk with Rabaut this morning. Is there any immediate danger?"

"No. I can play the game and handle safely—up to a certain point." Kerguelec hesitated. "Until, I think, we have left here. Other things have gone wrong, too; my private affairs. I've nothing left except to make sure the treasure does not reach Paris."

"It won't. Do you know his plans?"

"Vaguely. He's hinted at them. And something he said—nothing definite—made me afraid for you. I think he means——"

I laughed at this. "You think? But I know! Yes, he means to get rid of me. Never fear, I'll attend to that detail when the time comes! I'm keeping my eyes open."

"Good." Kerguelec smiled a little and put out a hand to mine. "I felt I had to warn you and tell you I'd not despise your help if needed. Good luck! Careful, now—let me slip out by myself. There's the chapel of the Trinity; I'll go by the bridge."

Kerguelec departed swiftly.

I remained a while in the church, staring down at the fragments of colored glass on the floor and wondering at the situation. The quiet balance of this girl wakened admiration in me. Handle Rabaut indeed! However, she might be able to manage it for the present. Once Rabaut got himself out of all danger and could turn to cold steel again, he would be a far different person to handle.

Naturally, I could make no plans. Any contingency might rise, and to see ahead was difficult in the extreme. My chief fear now was from Fromond, because my own escape depended on Rabaut's scheme going through, and I had unluckily given Fromond a hint that Rabaut was not to be trusted.

It was clear too how Rabaut had no intention of taking me from the Mont—yet I must somehow manage to leave with him. For my own sake, I could not turn on Rabaut and kill him, either now or later. He alone could, by virtue of his authority, effect the evasion; and merely to leave the Mont would do me little good. The whole fleet of France was centered on patrolling the western coasts in fear of an English descent, and only Rabaut could hope to win through and past this barrier. Nor could I impersonate the man, Rabaut being altogether too well-known for this to be managed.

"Well," I concluded with a shrug, "we'll have to trust to luck, wait for what turns up, and play the cards accordingly! Everything's on the knees of the gods just now. The devil of it is that I'm not at all indispensable to Rabaut, but he's quite indispensable to me! And in the meantime——"

I whirled suddenly, staring about. From somewhere had come a sharp, incoherent cry like the scream of a wild beast, instinct with startling emotions. It was in the voice of Fromond, and I thought it came from the west platform.

The great doors of the church opening on that platform were half closed, shutting off the place from my sight. I ran to them, then came out into the sunlight and halted.

Before me in the brightness stood a Fromond almost inarticulate with passion, shaken by convulsions of wild fury. For the moment I believe he was really beyond sanity. He stood shaking his clenched fists in air, trembling, and if ever the personal devil looked out of a man's face, it did then from his. The jeweler of Avranches had shrunk back out of the way in terror.

The object of Fromond's wrath was a bent black figure to my right—an infirm, limping priest who stood staring at him in silence, obviously amazed by the outbreak. The priest must have wandered up here from below in ignorance of the work going forward on the platform. Save for these three, it was empty.

Now from Fromond's lips poured a torrent of shrill abuse. I stepped forward with a sharp word to him and gestured the priest away, but he had not enough presence of mind to obey and stood gaping stupidly. Fromond whirled upon me rabidly; I had the impression that he was frothing at the lips. Before he could speak, his eyes drove past me and he stiffened, remained motionless. I turned my head and perceived three other figures coming out on the platform.

Two of them were soldiers—not our Alsatians, but local militia who knew and respected Fromond for a great man and scarce knew who I was. Between them walked the same old priest we had met in Pontaubault on the way here—he who had known Fromond from infancy. In a rush, I recalled his promise, knew he had come to give himself up, and attempted to take charge of matters and save the situation.

"Away with him!" I commanded the two soldiers. "Citizen Rabaut is not here—seek him in the abbot's rooms and lead this man——"

Fromond leaped suddenly, pushed me staggering to one side, and hurled a wild command at the two soldiers. They knew him, yet they hesitated. The old priest smiled and lifted his hand as though in benediction. Fromond struck it aside, caught him by the shoulder, and sent him reeling across the platform toward the verge.

The first priest, the lame one, uttered a cry of horror. Just in time, he darted out and caught the

198

older one, stopped him, brought to a halt two paces from the edge of the platform, beside the table. The two stood there waiting, fearful, yet with a strange dignity.

"Out of this, you fool!" Fromond shook his fist at me. "You dare to interfere and you'll go with them! Here, you men—shoot these cursed blackbirds!"

"Stop it!" I ordered, trying again to assert myself above this madman. "You men, listen to me— I'm the assistant commissioner from Paris. Take no orders from——"

As I spoke, I was getting out a pistol. It was loaded but unprimed. Fromond leaped at me, catlike, and struck it from my hand, I whipped in a blow to the face and sent him spinning, but there lay folly. Instantly the two soldiers were upon me. One tripped me up, the other sprawled on me as I lay; it was all done neatly, swiftly, and next instant I was helpless while Fromond shrilled out commands in a high, cracking voice.

My wrists were tied behind me, my ankles were lashed, and a dirty rag was wound about my mouth. Then I was jerked back and left to sit against the church door, while the two men picked up their muskets and inspected them, laughing. Fromond repeated his order to shoot, and turned to shake his fist at the two priests. The older one again lifted his hand and completed his benediction. His eyes seemed to drive Fromond mad; they were very sorrowful and not angry, as was his voice when he spoke.

"My poor son! I know it is not you who speaks —that dreadful injury in your youth——"

Fromond shrieked insanely, hurled himself forward, struck the priest across the face and actually knocked him backward from the platform. He was gone, over the fragments of the broken stone parapet—gone. Not so much as a cry came from the depths.

The other priest stood there, shaking in every limb, eyes closed. In this instant of horrified silence, holding even the two soldiers spellbound, his voice reached me. A portion of the requiem mass was upon his lips.

"*Ne absorbeat eas tartarus, ne cadant in obscurum, sed signifer sanctus Michael repraesentet eas in lucem——*"

With a strangled cry Fromond darted, struck him, hurled him out and away. One long, thin scream wailed up and was gone. For an instant I thought, and hoped, Fromond would follow his victims, but he recovered his balance and for a long moment remained gazing down at the sea. Then abruptly he staggered, turned, and half fell into the chair beside the table. Over it his face showed very white and terrible. He tried to speak, failed, but lifted his hand and pointed at me.

At this instant Rabaut appeared. One glance and he started forward. The two guards saluted stiffly, and Fromond screamed out at him in a burst of exultant rage.

"I sent them where they belong! Down to the sea with their whining prayers—down to the devil, if there is one! Keep your accursed priests away from here, Citizen Rabaut, or I'll send them all to the same place!"

Rabaut glanced at me, and I read a tacit warning in his eyes. Then he turned and regarded Fromond calmly, silently, and this look jerked sanity quickly back into the face of Fromond. After a moment Rabaut looked at the jeweler, still shrinking in horror, and cruelty twitched at his lips. He was minded to get all three of us out of the way, but the time had not come. He turned and came quietly to me, and jerked the filthy rag from my mouth.

"Steady, now," he warned, and snapped an order. One of the two guards came and loosed me, helping me to my feet. Rabaut took out his snuffbox and in his grand manner played with it in his fingers.

"We'd better get along with the inventory," he observed coldly, as though disdaining to go into recent events, and this air of his had a singularly quieting effect on Fromond. "Is this your pistol on the pavement, Citizen Martin? Better take care of it. To table, please!"

I picked up the weapon, and stumbled forward to the chair opposite Fromond. In no sense am I squeamish. Indian scalpings, battle-torn men, and the guillotine have all inured my senses to the sight of human life flitting, and in case of need I have not paused at the taking of a life or two myself—yet in this moment I was badly shaken up. The terrible sight of these murders transcended anything I had ever seen, and the thought was in my mind to take the devil opposite me by the throat and send him after his victims. I was checked by Rabaut, who coolly shoved the inventory into my hands.

"You may attend to this for me, Citizen Martin, at least temporarily. These lots of brass hearts— a tub of them, I see—are of no value, but they must be opened, as it is noted many of them contain enclosures, some of value. Perhaps you'll attend to

THE PAST CAUSES THE PRESENT

the opening, Citizen Fromond? And Citizen Plessis at his scales——"

Here appeared Pol Rouge and Pol Noir, and the other soldiers were sent whence they had come. The white-faced jeweler came up to the table and took his seat, not without one blinking grimace at the gulf below us. Fromond straightened up, wiped sweat from his thin face, then reached for a quill and leaned over his list.

Having thus started the machinery, Rabaut went to the side wall behind me and leaned there carelessly, watching us. Afterward, I could not but wonder at his thus remaining. Had he some prescience, some foreknowledge—but no! Impossible. He must have stayed only to make certain no trouble would arise between me and Fromond.

Gradually our silence gave place to low exchange of words, as we fell to work upon the votive hearts. Of these, several tubs stood around—one of gold, another of silver, others of baser metals; we chanced to begin on those of brass, as they stood first on the list.

These hearts, old and new across the centuries, were evidently the most favored ex-voto of the average pilgrim—and pilgrims had come by hundreds to this spot each year, from all over Europe.

SAINT MICHAEL'S GOLD

On each heart was displayed a flame or cross, capped by a crown of thorns and perhaps engraved with initials, names or dates. They opened like a watch, and contained either a writing, giving the object of the offering, or gifts. They were of no great value, save those studded with gems.

Fromond flung up a dozen to the table, opened them one by one, tossed away the contents, and passed them on to the jeweler; this latter was but slightly interested in the hearts of brass or copper, called in this part of Normandy 'gold of Villedieu.' Nothing of interest was retrieved from the interiors, until Fromond brought up a fresh lot from the tub.

Then, the first on which he put his hand seemed to startle him. He sat staring, his face slowly becoming whiter and whiter, until a veritable pallor of death was settled on that awry countenance of his. His fingers trembled. With an obvious effort, he forced the heart open and cast it to one side as he took the objects from it. I looked at the heart, and on one side saw certain letters and a date engraved:

J. F.
29 Septembre, 1751

THE PAST CAUSES THE PRESENT

It came to me that these were the initials of Jacques Fromond.

I watched. Rabaut, aware of something unusual, came up to the table. The jeweler sat petrified with terror by the face of Fromond, who stared at the things in his hand. One of these was a long curl of yellow hair, the fine soft floss of a child, tied about with a blue ribbon. The other was a curled strip of parchment, and this the fingers of Fromond opened and spread out upon the table. The quivering fingers held it there, yet the eyes did not see it. They had closed, those pale blue, terrible eyes; the man was as though gripped by an ague, trembling in every limb.

I leaned forward. The writing on the parchment was upside down to me, yet it was very clear and distinct, easily deciphered. It revealed to me, to all of us, a frightful thing:

"Claude Fromond et Jeanne Courtois, époux, ont offerts ce coeur à l'Archange Saint Michel qui préserva miraculeusement leur enfant, Jacques, victim d'un accident affreux. Que le prince des Milices Célestes protège à jamais leur fils chéri."

Or, as the inscription would read put into English words:

SAINT MICHAEL'S GOLD

"Claude Fromond and Jeanne Courtois, his wife, have offered this heart to the Archangel St. Michael, who miraculously preserved their child, Jacques, victim of a terrible accident. May the Prince of the Heavenly Cohorts ever protect their dear son!"

Thus before us lay clear the threads of a dark and terrible history, the more so when the eyes of Fromond opened and looked down at the paper before him.

Slowly, mechanically, one hand lifted and the groping, shaking fingers sought the old injury on the left side of his head. Forty years ago—why, I could see the awful thing, and the hell of it, full-fledged there in his face! He must have remembered it all, the pilgrimage his parents had made here, bare-footed, how they had vowed their hurt son to the service of Saint Michael should he recover from the hurt, how they had returned home to find the boy recovering. And then, the years afterward——

The whole body of Fromond seemed to jerk suddenly; one hand clutched at the brass heart. The table was shoved back upon us as his other hand spurned it. A cry burst from him, the most mournful and soul-piercing cry ever I heard from human lips—a cry filled with things unutterable, with a

206

THE PAST CAUSES THE PRESENT

heartbreak of remorse beyond all words, with emotions inexpressible.

Fromond came to his feet. He swayed before us a moment and gasped out something incoherent; then he turned about and took two swift steps to the edge of the platform. Rabaut started forward too late. One convulsive tremor shook Fromond from head to foot. Lifting both arms, that same unforgettable cry coming again to his lips like the wail of a lost soul, he leaped straight out—was gone. Only the echo of his cry came up to us, and then trailed away into thin silence.

I staggered to my feet, feeling a little sick.

The soldiers were staring, white-faced. The little Norman jeweler had fallen face down across the table in a dead faint. Rabaut strode out to the verge of the gulf and stood there a long moment, gazing downward, until at length he turned about and regarded me with his cynical calm, unmoved.

"At last," he observed reflectively, taking out his snuffbox and snapping the lid, "at last, my dear Martin, we may begin to understand Jacques Fromond."

And from this instant, too, seeing more clearly the coldly inhuman soul of Rabaut, I began to fear him.

CHAPTER X

NOTHING happens in this little world without exerting a far-reaching ripple of effect upon apparently unrelated matters. Thus the events culminating in the suicide of Fromond exerted an immediate and singular influence upon me, and indeed upon all of us, since they completely altered the whole course of later happenings.

A keenly disturbing factor was removed. The presence of this man, somewhat irresponsible and liable to real or assumed outbursts of frenzy at any instant, I think must have been holding us all more or less irresolute. To give the devil his due, here was a strong personality, one by no means to be shoved into the background, but to be sharply reckoned with. His abrupt removal from our midst was

REFUGE IS NOT ALWAYS SAFETY

far more than a mere wiping away of possible obstruction and danger. It instantly flung each of us upon his own active resources and gave an impetus to private schemes.

So far as I was concerned, it brought abrupt wakening to hard facts. Until this moment I had been quite content to wait idly, lulled by the smoothness with which everything was pressing forward to my own advantage, and finding a perilous satisfaction in playing a game of wits. The fates were auspicious and heads were better than hands.

Now however I was jerked face to face with cold reality. The losing player of this game encountered death, sudden and merciless. Life was cheap here as in Paris itself, murder as imminent, and survival was possible only to him who struck first and hardest with unsparing hand. Nothing but a cold and pitiless strength, grinding down and mounting upon all in the way, could hope to ride the wave.

If this realization drove home to me, it also reached Rabaut at the same instant and wakened him to his old self. He had been in check before Fromond, who was a menace to his plans, but now he was freed and supreme in authority except for the American whom he believed his dupe. Fromond was gone, very opportunely, and he at once seized

upon the chance to get rid of the remaining menace—the Norman jeweler-spy. The way he did it
too was characteristic of Rabaut at his best.

Before the jeweler had recovered from his faint
and lifted his pallid face from the table, Rabaut was
taking possession of the chair so recently vacated
by Fromond. He was all cold authority personified.

"Citizen Martin!" He pushed quills and ink-pot
over to me. "You will write down what has happened here, in brief detail. Paper of the committee—good! I'll be writing an official summary."

The jeweler and the soldiers stared, and no wonder. This inhuman coolness of Rabaut's was ter-
rifying; it gave me, more than the others, a glimpse
of the actual man, for I alone had some inkling of
his purpose.

The quills scratched. I wrote briefly and to the
point concerning Fromond's death, and when I had
finished, Rabaut asked me to read it aloud. He then
beckoned forward the two soldiers, who took quills
and made their mark as witnesses—neither could
write. The paper then went to the jeweler who
signed it and passed it back. Rabaut shook his head
and delivered his verbal bomb with a slight smile.

"No, no, citizen, keep it! At low tide this evening you will go to Pontorson for the night. In

the morning, you'll go on to Avranches. There you will lay this report and my own before the committee of public safety, requesting them to appoint another delegate in the place of Citizen Fromond— a delegate of upright and conscientious integrity. You'll accompany him back here and then resume the task."

"But, citizen commissioner!" faltered the jeweler, who had no liking for the journey or the delay in putting his gold into the pot. "It is a journey, this! And dangerous——"

"And those are my orders," said Rabaut, and flung me a sly glance. "Since it is dangerous, take four men of the militia here as your escort. Vive la République!"

The jeweler acquiesced, as he needs must, though none too happily. Rabaut, ordering the two grenadiers to return the treasure to its own place, rose.

"So, for the moment, we lay aside the task," he said lightly. "Citizen Martin, shall we take a turn on the terraces above? The view from there, they say, is superb."

I assented.

In ten minutes, the two of us were strolling about the terraces at the crest of the abbey. A magnificent panorama was unrolled before us—the long stretch of coast with its sand-dunes and dotted towers, dim Granville across the water, the wide bay to the west, Tombelaine ruined and deserted, Mount Dol rising blue-green to the south. Presently Rabaut chuckled and made pretense of opening his mind to me.

"Beautiful, is it not, how things fit into our plan? The jeweler reaches Avranches tomorrow. Next day he will return, bringing a man to take Fromond's place—bringing also, no doubt, the delayed letters from Paris. You comprehend?"

"You are staking everything on tomorrow night, then?"

"Everything—for us both, Martin! Tomorrow I pick out all the gold to take with us; Pol Rouge and Pol Noir will pouch it safely. Four of the local militia will be gone. Our four Alsatians will replace them, having the guard tomorrow night. Thus we shall be able to get away unmolested. The Alsatians will not understand, but they'll not dare offer any objections to my orders."

"Things seem to fall your way," I observed. "What if the lugger does not come?"

"Since things fall my way, she cannot fail."

I hazarded a bold stroke, to draw him into the open.

REFUGE IS NOT ALWAYS SAFETY

"And the Breton, this Kerguelec?"

Rabaut halted and turned, his smiling grimace on his lips.

"Martin, I'll tell you something—show you how things fall my way. As that dragoon captain in Pontorson said this Breton is an émigré, a noble disguised. Well, I have given Kerguelec the chance to go with us and take a share in the treasure; he has agreed. In case we are stopped by any English ship, we become émigrés—he a de Rohan, I a St.-Servaut—fleeing with our personal belongings to America. We'll not be molested; rather, we'll be aided! You comprehend? The whole scheme falls in perfectly, without a flaw. A third of the treasure awaits you—eh?"

"Thank you, I want none of it," I responded curtly. To myself, I smiled at this effort to bribe me—the second offer of the sort in the same day, both offers with the treasure still unwon!

"Bah! Money is always useful to have these days," said Rabaut carelessly. I think he disbelieved my protest, for he made no further comment upon it. Nor did I make any comment on his tissue of half-truths regarding Kerguelec. "The lugger," he resumed, "should arrive off the Mont tomorrow night, sometime before midnight. I ordered her to show two lights, one above the other, as a signal. It will be dark toward ten o'clock. Our two Parisians will carry down the gold in the sacks——"

"Openly?" I objected. Rabaut shrugged.

"Why not, eh? These thick-skulled peasants will suspect nothing—they have the capacity for wonder, but not the ability to reason! By the time they or anyone else realized that Citizen Commissioner Rabaut has decamped with St. Michael's gold, that same citizen will be out of the bay and at sea—and let the devil stop him! So, then, agreed?"

I nodded, and we descended from the terraces.

Before dark that evening the jeweler and four of the local guards set out afoot for Pontorson, where they would secure horses. No search was made for the bodies of Fromond or the two priests—the tide would attend to them in its own good time. Besides, Fromond was not greatly mourned by anyone and had, I gathered, no family.

Talking with Rabaut that night, and Kerguelec, we discussed squarely the scheme for getting away. Rabaut was exultant and confident. When I set forth practical objections, such as the unlikelihood of the lugger being provisioned and watered for

REFUGE IS NOT ALWAYS SAFETY

such a voyage, he broke into a chuckle and tapped my arm.

"Look you! One advantage in being a commissioner is that his orders are unquestioned. So then, I ordered. The lugger will be well enough provisioned for a voyage to Dominique—and if to the Antilles, then to America also! Have no fear. He who travels with Citizen Rabaut is well taken care of."

"And who sups with the devil needs a long spoon," I retorted, and left them. "Good night to you both! I'm for bed."

So I was, indeed, but not to any peaceful slumber, being tormented with visions of Fromond plunging down that fearful descent, clutching still in his hand the little heart of brass.* It happened repeatedly, this dream, but the last time with a difference. In his fall, his eyes seemed to turn upon me, vivid blue and burning with hatred, and I heard his voice calling to me in a shrill cry.

"Beware of the night! Beware of the night! Beware of the dawn!"

So vivid was it, I came all awake with the sound ringing in my ears. Though I pretend to no belief

---

* This heart was retrieved by a fisherman in 1811.

SAINT MICHAEL'S GOLD

in dreams, I do not laugh at what is past my comprehension; for, it seems to me if we understood everything in the two worlds we should be on a level with the Supreme Being, and no longer mere mortals.

So for a little while I lay awake, profoundly startled and uneasy. Then I broke into a cold sweat at hearing a sound—someone was here in my room, in the darkness! Ashamed of my terrors, fully awake, I sat up with a laugh.

"Well? Who is it?"

"Quiet! I, Kerguelec. Where are you?"

"Near the window."

Without a sound Kerguelec approached the huge bed, guided by my voice. Presently his hand found mine and gripped it, and he sat on the wooden side of the structure. I knew, of course, something had gone wrong.

"What's the matter—anything urgent?"

"What can be more urgent than death?" The Breton laughed, a weary bitterness in his voice. "Had I reached here a week earlier, I would have beaten death, but I failed. However—I'm here on your errand, not my own."

These half mysterious, half sad words puzzled me, until I recollected all Kerguelec's mentions of

216

private business at the Mont—and my refusals to enter into it. Somehow, I knew, he had encountered a keen disappointment.

"What is it, Kerguelec?" I said quietly. "I've long since regretted my brusque refusal to listen to you at the first. If there's anything I can do now ——"

"There's nothing," he said, and pressed my hand slightly. "No, Martin, it would have done no good in any case. I've failed—let it go! I had to reach you at once, for your own sake. Do you know what Rabaut plans?"

"As regards me? Not in detail, but I can guess."

"It's early yet, before midnight. Rabaut is down below, on the Inner Degree, with Pol Rouge and Pol Noir and one of the Alsatians. Their voices carried up the walls so that I could hear every word. He's ordered them to seize you at dawn."

"At dawn!" I repeated in dismay. The words of my dream flashed again to my mind. "Odd! Fromond said——"

I told of the dream on which I had wakened. Kerguelec dismissed it impatiently.

"Let be—the danger presses. The scheme is to arrest you and leave you here. Rabaut hopes to get off tomorrow night; you'll remain as a scapegoat on whom the committee can take vengeance."

This information held me startled and aghast. Sly Rabaut! He had flung me off guard indeed by seeming to take me into his confidence and detailing his plans. I had anticipated no attempt against me until the following night at the earliest —until his own escape was well assured.

"Then there's only one course to take," I said. "I'll have to see him at once, for only a bold front can carry the day now. To hide would be sheer folly, to fight, sheer madness. Flight is utterly impossible. If I face him down, threaten to give away his fine schemes, I may force him to postpone matters until later——"

"No, no!" broke in Kerguelec swiftly. "That's out of the question; he would only trap you tomorrow somehow—remember, he holds all the cards! I have a better plan, and the only one offering any hope."

"Good. Name it."

"The tide is in, and a thick fog has come with it. There's your only chance. You know about the lugger coming tomorrow night? I know how you may make it."

"Aboard her, you mean?"

"Yes, I'll take your cloak and hat now, up to the

west platform where everything happened this afternoon. I'll leave them there by the edge. It will be
thought you've fallen over when your absence is
discovered."

"And where'll I be?" I inquired drily.

"Pursuing folly, as you termed it—in hiding!
You'll have to get out of here, down to the town,
and out; that's for you to manage, but the fog is
thick and will help you. Get outside the walls and
remain until dawn, when the tide will be at ebb.
Then pass around on the west side of the Mont.
Just above the water there you'll find the ruins of
a small chapel under the cliff. A stairway used to
go down to it from the abbey, but that is long ago
ruined and gone—the only access is around the
shore. You can hide there, and no one will suspect."

Kerguelec poured all this out in a breath.

"Very well," I assented, trying to grapple with
the scheme. "But to what end?"

"When the ship comes tomorrow night, swim off
to her—oh, I know it sounds desperate," went on
the Breton wearily, "yet I can think of nothing else!
And it is less desperate than to think of pitting
yourself against Rabaut here, where he has everything to aid him, and you nothing!"

"It's extremely cheerful, this prospect of yours!"

219

I observed with a curt laugh. "The ship may be a mile or two off the island——"

"Listen! There are a dozen things to favor you —I know the place, you see. But we've no time to talk further," broke in Kerguelec. "I had to let you know all this at once. If you can get aboard the boat, things may be very different—you'll have a chance to catch Rabaut unprepared. Until we get away from here, we don't dare touch him—you see? All depends on him, that far. Hurry now! You must act at once, now, while the fog is thick! Give me any papers or other things you want taken care of."

My hesitation was brief. Now thoroughly awake, I could perceive the urgency of the errand bringing Kerguelec here, and his plan was tempting. It was illogical and insane, true, yet I was in no position to argue probabilities. The strait was desperate. There was a slim chance to make Rabaut think I had fallen from the platform during the night. Whether I could get outside the walls undiscovered, even with the help of the fog, was a large question, and to get aboard the lugger by swimming seemed rank folly.

"Beggars can't be choosers," I said. "Stay where you are, now. I'll dress and give you my papers and money."

REFUGE IS NOT ALWAYS SAFETY

In five minutes I had struggled into my clothes. The room was in pitch blackness and was chokily damp with fog. The idea of giving up hat and cloak was unpleasant until I recollected the wardrobe filled with moldering garments of former tenants. Feeling about, I soon obtained a thick fustian cassock with cowl and donned it. Then I came back to the bedside, my few belongings ready.

"Here you are—cloak, hat, money and papers," I said, putting them into the hands of Kerguelec. "And thanks for your warning, my friend! Unless Rabaut lied, the lugger is to show two lights, and I should make her well enough. If not, and if things go amiss, I'll say goodby to you now. Sure you're not in any danger?"

"Not at present." Kerguelec's fingers pressed mine warmly. "Keep a stout heart, comrade! I'll have pistols ready for you tomorrow night. If things go wrong, I'll kill Rabaut and we'll make for the shore—we'll have a chance to make the Vendée, at worst. Things are not at such crisis yet, even if I have failed dismally."

"Failed? Not you," I returned. Kerguelec laughed a little, sadly.

"Ah, but you don't know! I learned something yesterday—however, no bothering you with my af-

221

fairs now. It's ended, and we'll look forward to tomorrow night, eh? God keep you, comrade!"

"And you," I answered, more than a little puzzled by Kerguelec's words.

The room fell into silence—the Breton was gone with scarce a sound.

I stepped out into the corridor and just in time caught a sound on the stairs. It was Rabaut, groping his way along with many a curse on the black fog. He came up and went to his own chamber. While he was there trying to make a light, I stole past his doorway and down the stairs. I was quite unarmed, for pistols were of no use in this emergency, when a shot would discover everything. Leaving my pistols in the room, too, would make my supposed death much more convincing.

It must be confessed I was not half in love with the job ahead. When at length I came down to the level of the Inner Degree and stepped out into that cañon of masonry, I stood overcome by a sense of futility. It was exactly as though I stood at the bottom of a vast well, the walls on every side collecting the dampness and dripping continually. The blackness was complete. I could only hope to reach the Chatelet, a few paces distant, by groping my way.

REFUGE IS NOT ALWAYS SAFETY

If the Chatelet, the only tiny opening in this huge pile of granite, were closed and barred, I might as well turn back. However I guessed it was seldom closed, the portcullis never dropped, for the watch in this place was extremely slack. No danger was felt from the prisoners, and if they wished to escape, they were welcome to the chance of death. The Mont was far better defended by its natural situation than by any work of human hands, so far as any escape or any external attack was concerned.

I slowly moved downward, came at last to a firm level of stone flagging, and then descried a glimmer of light off to the left, where was the guardroom. Low voices reached me, the fragrant odor of tobacco, and then the clack of wooden sabots on stone. I flattened against the wall and waited.

"Bah! Don't be a fool," growled a rough voice. "Those accursed Alsatians are out of the way, and the Parisians also, and the commissioner's gone to bed. We can slip down to the Licorne, get the wine, and be back here in no time. Who's going to bother us on a dog's night like this?"

"Come along then," was the response. "It's your money, so lead the way!"

The sabots clattered, and then began to slap on descending stairs, so I knew the two men of the guard were gone ahead of me, down toward town. The light remained in the guardroom, and I made my way to it.

As I had already guessed, it came from a little blaze in the huge fireplace. Before it lying on outspread cloaks were a pack of cards and two large packets of food, bread and cheese; these latter I took and stowed away in my pockets beneath the monk's robe. Then I went to the Chatelet, passed the low portal and down the steep stairs, and so down the length of the curving Outer Degree, until I reached the sweeping ascent from the town below.

Once out here in open air, I could realize the clammy thickness of the fog—fully as thick as the one so nearly destroying me on our first approach to the Mont. To feel one's way down the steep hill with its many landings and flights of stairs was a matter requiring caution.

At least the black robe served me well, and only a few moments later proved its utility when I heard the sabot-clatter of the two guards returning. They went back up the hill, passing me almost within touching distance, yet my presence was not guessed, nor could I see them.

Gaining confidence at this, I went on down at better speed and presently sighted, at a distance of some few feet, the dim yellow glow of light in the windows of the Licorne Rouge, where Pol Rouge and Pol Noir were lustily shouting bawdy ballads. On past this, to the Porte du Roi, a solid black mass barricading the street. Here the postern was open and unguarded, so I continued without molestation to the outer gate beyond. This was closed, and a group of guards sat about a small fire in the courtyard.

Here I was blocked, and sat down to cool my heels in obscurity, for while I might gain the walls it would be impossible to descend from them without a rope. In any case, so long as the fog and tide held, I could not hope to pass around by the shore to the ruined chapel, much less ascertain where the place was.

However, fortune favored me. By the talk I learned the guards were expecting some overdue fishermen belonging to the place, and presently they set alight a huge flaring cresset above the gate. A number of women, also expecting the missing men, came down to the barbican and lined the walls. Some little while afterward we heard a faint hail from outside.

At once men began to shout, drums were set beating, and two muskets banged off, and after a time the missing fishermen found their way to the gate, which had been flung open.

They entered, and a great time was had by all in French fashion, with general embracing and much loud talk. Under cover of this confusion, I calmly shouldered my way through the group, unnoticed in the density of fog, and so got out of the gate before it was closed again. And there I stayed, for I had no mind to go splashing among rocks and quick-sands in pitch blackness.

All this alarm and firing would later render my own disappearance more inexplicable, it was clear, and would lend color to the theory of my death. Rabaut would know the watch had been on the alert, and he would probably be glad to consider me out of his way, whether dead or in hiding. Things, as he said, fell his way—let him continue in the theory!

Outside the walls was a sharp cluster of rocks and a little beach where a few boats were drawn up. I settled down beside a boat, pulled up the cowl of my robe, and went to sleep, though fitfully. When I wakened, it was to a chill touch of breeze, and I came stiffly to my feet.

The tide was going out, dawn was close at hand, and a light wind was sending the fog-vapors swirling and eddying up about the walls and pinnacles above. It was high time to be off, so I started around to the western, or seaward, face of the Mont. In ten minutes I was past the walls and beneath the steep rock scarp, towering bald and bare into the sky.

Daylight was increasing and the mist was now going out fast. Soon, rounding a projection of the rocky mass, I came in sight of my objective—a tiny tongue of rock on which stood a small square building, partly in ruins but still roofed over. Above it a steep slope strewn with trees led on to the abbey walls, here impenetrable and naked, towering far and high. No battlements were needed for defense on this side of the island.

Sunrise touched the sky with gold as I reached the tiny promontory and clambered up to the ruins above, my robe flung back for freedom of action. Before me appeared a doorless opening, and I looked into what had once been a tiny chapel, now littered with the débris of destruction. With a sigh of relief I got out of my black robe and started into the place.

Next instant ten long fingers had me by the throat.

CHAPTER XI

THE interior of the little ruined chapel was yet dim and obscure—the full day had not yet broken. By good luck I had let go the black monk's robe, and I had some freedom to grapple with those terrible fingers.

They had reached to me from behind, and now sank into my throat like steel claws. The silence of it was unnerving for an instant, then the touch of human flesh put strength into me. A hot breath beat upon my neck, and I tried to twist about, to see with whom I was fighting, but in vain.

Desperate, frantic under the throttling grip, I stooped and tried to fling my assailant over my head. He evaded; all his weight descended on my back and he had me like an old man of the sea, legs twined about my thighs, fingers digging into my throat. I staggered forward a pace or two—reaching back, smashing blindly at the body clinging to me—

then jerked up my head sharply. Struck full in the mouth, my savage attacker loosened his grip with a cry.

I had him then—had him in a wrenching grip about the shoulders. We were twined like two snakes, lost balance, came heavily to the floor together. He tried to fight back, until I got home one blow in the face; and, singularly enough, this finished him. Abruptly, all the strength seemed to go out of him. He fell limp, motionless, yet lay gazing up at me with queerly haunting eyes.

Poised on one knee above him, I stared down as I gulped the air into my lungs. A slender figure, this, clad in tattered black garments, ill-smelling and foul, much emaciated. Almost the first glance gave the explanation—this man must be one of the unhappy priests from the dungeons above, probably an escaped prisoner. His long hair was gray-streaked, his face half-concealed by a stubble of beard, yet something familiar in this face held my gaze and puzzled me.

"Well, you've taken me," he said in a tone of resignation. "Had my strength lasted, it had been another story! Call them in and get it over with."

"Faith, I believe you!" I said, feeling my throat. His brief spasmodic strength had been furious.

Drawing back from him, I put out my hand. "Come, sit up! If you had spoken before grappling me, my friend, you'd have saved us both a bit of hard work."

"Eh?"

He sat up, staring at me with blank incredulity. Undoubtedly he had taken me for a searcher, not stopping to ask of me or of his own reason.

"I'm not looking for you—I'm looking for shelter," I said quietly. "Surely I've seen you before—in Paris, perhaps? Something about your face ——"

He shook his head, and wiped blood from his lips where my stroke had cut them.

"No," he said dully. "No."

"You're an évadé—from up above?"

He nodded. "The damnable water up above! It's foul. It breeds fever. I've had nothing to eat for two days—good water here. I hoped to get away to the coast—impossible. *Diable!* It's no hospitable tavern, this!"

He broke off abruptly. I searched his face frowningly—odd language, this, for a priest! And surely I should know him, for something in those oval, regular features struck to my memory. His necessity struck more sharply, and I hauled from my pocket one of the stolen meals I had brought from the guardroom, blessing the chance that had flung it my way.

"Here's bread and cheese—a meal for us both now, and another like it tonight," I said. "Set your teeth into this, and we can talk later on."

His eyes burned ravenously, yet he restrained himself while I divided the hunks of bread and cheese. His gaze dwelt upon me wonderingly, half fearfully, until I shoved his portion at him. Then he smiled.

"Thank you, monsieur. May I offer my apologies for the reception tendered you?"

"Balanced by my damage to your face," I said, and laughed.

I brought in my monk's robe, at which he looked sharply, and sat on it. In five minutes our meal had disappeared. It was dry eating, and when I said as much, my companion smiled and beckoned me to a crypt below the chapel. Here he bent above a tiny trickle of water, drinking, and motioned me to it.

"This is the old chapel of St. Aubert, and the spring is not very good, but it is good enough."

He went back above. When I returned there, I found him on his knees, and did not disturb his devotions. Presently he rose and came to me, smiling, hand outstretched.

"Monsieur, I am in your debt for an excellent meal! You are one of the priests from up above, then?"

"I? Not at all. You have the advantage of me there——"

"But I'm no priest!" he ejaculated, then laughed. We broke into joint laughter, and he explained. "I was escaping, used the clothes of a priest—it was my only chance. The Blues would have deported me with the other priests, but I fell ill and they brought me here instead. Naturally I could not change back——"

Here then was some aristocrat whose head had been momentarily saved by his priestly disguise. Yet surely I had seen him somewhere ere this, and said as much.

"Your face is certainly known to me—you've been in Paris?"

"No, in prison. I am Louis de Rohan—titles are gone, but names cannot be destroyed."

I was speechless for an instant. De Rohan! No wonder his face looked familiar.

"There is a Marie de Rohan up above," I said. "A relative?"

A FOE MAY PROVE TO BE A BROTHER

"Marie—my sister? Impossible!" he cried sharply. "For the love of heaven, monsieur, are you joking?"

I calmed his swift agitation, drew him into a corner, made myself comfortable, and went at the business of explanation. Amazing as this meeting appeared, it soon showed itself quite natural. If men do not distort them, human events often have a way of working themselves out in startling yet logical fashion, unless one prefers to admit the element of divine guidance.

Here I had, in the presence of de Rohan, the reason for Kerguelec's mysterious words about a personal errand—the reason, indeed, behind more than words! Secrets were few in these days, information was the easiest of all things to be obtained, and word of de Rohan's plight had got out of France to his friends. So the girl had undertaken a desperate errand—partly for the king, partly for the sake of her brother in Mont St. Michel.

"This, then, is why she insisted on coming here and refused to get away!" I commented. De Rohan nodded eager, excited assent, though he did not yet know the story. "And now she's heard of your supposed death—you must be the priest who tried to escape and fell into the sea, eh? Only a few days ago?"

"Undoubtedly. I was down with fever when the chance came, but could not miss it."

So he recounted his evasion. One of the immured priests had chanced upon a great coil of rope, stored away and forgotten and somewhat rotted. De Rohan risked it, lowering himself from one of the cells to the wooded scarp just above us. The rope broke. He sustained a bad fall and barely managed to creep into this ruined chapel before collapsing. No search had been made, for it was supposed he had fallen into the sea.

Since then he had hoped nightly to steal away and make the coast, thence the Vendée. His shaking-up had been too severe, however, and fever returned upon him, robbing him of strength. His little supply of food gave out. Except for the fog which brought me here, he would have tried to crawl to the coast during the past night; the fog had checked him, as though destiny were determined to hold him to his fate.

"Perhaps it was God, too," he concluded. "Why not? What seems destruction turns out to be help and salvation."

"Well, you've a choice ahead," I observed, when

he had talked himself out and given me full comprehension of the situation. "Tonight, if you like, you can try for the coast——"

"With Marie up above?" he exclaimed. "No, no, my friend! Still, I do not entirely comprehend what is afoot——"

I laughed grimly, in sudden recollection. I understood everything, he did not. The poor man had gained the sketchiest notion of the affair from my few words, and no doubt his head was in a whirl.

"Why," I said, "your sister is not alone—she is with a man, noble like yourself, the Marquis de St.-Servaut——"

De Rohan leaped to his feet. Into his sallow, half-bearded features came a dark flush and ebbed away.

"He—that devil! Impossible! It was he who betrayed me, who denounced my poor brother and caused his death——"

"And who now," I said, "thrusts his advances upon your sister and intends to take her with him to America. If you can quiet down, I'll explain."

Often enough in Paris I had seen the temper of the old aristocracy when put to the test, yet never more clearly than in this moment. Faced with such news as must have pierced to his very soul, this poor fugitive became transformed. His agitation vanished. He quietly seated himself and regarded me with a gaze composed and clear. The same composure showed in his voice, by far more difficult of control than the features, when he replied.

"You interest me, monsieur. Will you have the goodness to continue?"

I would and did. In a short while I had made him conversant with the entire situation; he listened in silence, only a slight flash of his eyes betraying any emotion. Beneath this haggard countenance was now emerging the inner man, resolute, unflinching, keenly alert. When I had finished my exposition, he nodded quietly.

"I understand, monsieur. You are offering me the chance of accompanying you tonight?"

"If you want it, yes," and I shrugged. "I warn you, however, it's a desperate, even a mad, risk! To swim off to that——"

"I can swim well," he rejoined. "Further, it's not so mad as it may seem—we'll find the water very warm, because of its shallow depth and the day-hot sand. And if we make the lugger, I'll be of use. I was in the navy in the old days, had my own ship——"

"So that's what Kerguelec meant about finding a

236

A FOE MAY PROVE TO BE A BROTHER

seaman to aid us!" I exclaimed. "Well, you know the risk, de Rohan——"

"And accept it. Shall we keep any watch today?"

"Useless. If we are found, we have no way of escape."

"Then let us sleep, against the fatigue of to-night!"

I nodded. In one corner he had a sorry couch of seaweed and rags and his rotten shreds of rope; with my monk's robe added, at least the chill of the bare stones was obviated. We shared this excuse for a pallet, and in ten minutes I was sound asleep.

My wakening came in late afternoon. It came suddenly, abruptly, to a man's rough and full-throated laugh.

Sitting up, I stared around blankly, for the moment bewildered, finding only emptiness and silence about me. Through my head were running wild memories—Fromond's frightful end, the narrow-eyed, cynical face of Rabaut, the soft voice of an unmasked Kerguelec. Perhaps the laughter had been a vagary of dream, then——

A shadow, noiseless, slipped through the doorway. De Rohan stood before me, hand to lips, and spoke under his breath.

"Careful! Two fishermen from the Mont outside. The tide is down. They are coming in here shortly—they said so."

I leaped up. "Now?"

"Presently. They're resting just below."

Emphasizing his words, came another laugh and a rumble of voices.

"Weapons?" I asked.

"None. We can evade them by going down into the crypt—better to tie them up."

"Why?"

"They have nets—you comprehend? We can use those poles tonight."

I was slow to comprehend, not knowing the local customs. It seemed the fishermen of the coast carried a pair of long, light poles with net strung between. With these, they waded along and scraped the bottom yards in advance. When de Rohan had explained, I saw at once how excellently those poles would fit in our haphazard scheme of things.

"By all means. But how? You're unable to fight——"

"Trust me for my share!" and de Rohan laughed. "Besides, they're old men, Montois, and will be too frightened to put up a fight."

I shrugged. Here was a different creature from the shaggy, pallid wreck of a man who had flung

himself upon me when I entered the chapel! Energy
gleamed in his dark eyes, and the blurred outlines of
his face showed hard, clear-cut, beneath the bearded
mask.

"Get behind the doorway, then."

We took position on either side the entrance. A
broken stone in the wall close by caught my eye.
Working at it, I loosened a jagged fragment six
inches in length, peered out, and then passed it to
de Rohan. He took it with a nod of satisfaction.

The rough voices came to us, closer now—bare
feet made no noise. Exchanging some rude jest,
the two fishermen stooped and entered the place,
blinking. They were gnarled men of perhaps fifty
years—everyone in the west of France within the
draft age was either in the army or gone to the
Vendée—but were sturdy fellows, roughly dressed,
shaggy-bearded.

De Rohan launched himself, grappled with the
nearer man, and dragged him to the floor. I took
the other from behind as he turned—caught him
with one full-weight blow behind the ear and sent
him headlong across the place, senseless. I darted
to help de Rohan, and found his stone had done the
trick. Both men were sprawled unconscious upon
the floor, and my companion rose with a smile.

SAINT MICHAEL'S GOLD

"Tie them up, eh? Bits of this rope will serve——"

We went to work with lengths of the rope, having taken two excellent long knives from our captives, and presently had the hapless Montois trussed and laid away in a dark corner. Inspection of the spoils showed, besides the knives, some bread and cheese of dubious quality, and two flasks half filled with red wine, also some tobacco which I welcomed gladly.

Our prisoners were placed face to wall, where they could see nothing of us. Upon recovering, they demanded to know who had thus assaulted honest men, but after a curse or two obeyed my order and fell silent. So they remained during the rest of the afternoon, while I smoked their tobacco and enjoyed life.

Later, when the first shades of evening gathered about the Mont, de Rohan slipped outside and returned with the nets, left standing by the rock. These we stripped from the poles and then bound the latter firmly together, pair by pair, put the pairs together, and thus had between us a long, awkward, but highly sustaining float. We might have need of it, if compelled to be in the water a great length of time.

A FOE MAY PROVE TO BE A BROTHER

We made a very comfortable meal off our captured provender and wine, while the two prisoners
groaned dismally but in vain. De Rohan was im-
mensely heartened by the food and drink, and already his weakness was in great part dispelled.

"You'll not leave them to rot here, I suppose?"
he asked, with a gesture toward our captives.

"No," I said. "When we get off, I'll cut their
ankles free—they'll get home all right in the course
of the night, but will have to wait here for the tide
to fall. Without fire, they can't attract any attention from above—this is the blank side of the walls,
too, so it's safe enough. How's the weather?"

"Excellent."

We left the shelter and from the lip of the tiny
rock promontory inspected the darkling waters before us. The tide was coming in rapidly, the night
was clear and starry, and at our backs rose the
Mont, a gloomy mass bulking against the sky without a light showing.

An hour or more we sat there, talking between
ourselves, and in this short while de Rohan and I
became measureably well acquainted. There was
good steel in the man. He was none of your flaunt-
ing, idle aristocrats; he had been bred to the navy
and before the revolution burst had commanded a

frigate. What was rarer too he could see with my own eye when it came to his native folk.

"Fight for the boy in the Temple? Not I," he declared with conviction. "It would not be for him, in any case, but for those rogues of princes, who are pawns in the hand of Prussia and England! They stay in safety and let lesser men shed their blood. For France I would fight, yes; but not for those cowards. France is now a republic, and to fight for the royal cause is to fight against France under the orders of foreigners—no, no! We Rohans are not poor folk. We have money laid aside in England. If I ever get safely away, I may go to America, where so many others have fled, and there take up a new life without any back glances on a foundered past."

"You'll not have much choice in the matter," I said drily. "Either we die tonight, or else we get away—on the trail to America! First, however, we'll have to slip past the French fleet, for they're watching the whole coast."

"Aye, and there's the rub," he assented. "Look you, Martin! What's to prevent our going now around the shore to the barbican gate and waiting there until Rabaut sets off—then knifing him and his men and setting out? Nothing, except the fleet

A FOE MAY PROVE TO BE A BROTHER

of France! Every league of coast is watched, both against émigrés and against a landing of the English. An alarm beacon from the Mont, here, would be flashed to St. Malo and Granville, on to Brest and Cherbourg—we'd never get out of the bay of Cancale! And who could pass through the fleet except Rabaut?"

"Precisely," and I nodded. "We can only hope to get aboard that lugger somehow—and we must do it ahead of Rabaut. Then he'll be at our mercy. Either this, or else slip aboard her unseen. To tell the truth, the whole affair is so hazy, so dependent on circumstances, it would be mere folly to try and plan out any course of action."

"Right. Then you're in command, Monsieur Martin!" he said cheerfully. "I'm entirely in your hands, and you may count on me to obey your orders implicitly."

"In that case," and I stood up, "suppose you get our float launched."

"Eh? Do we start now?"

I pointed to a faint glitter among the stars, to seaward.

"Our lugger. Two lights, one above the other. When Rabaut will leave the Mont we don't know, but probably not for some time yet. Let's go."

SAINT MICHAEL'S GOLD

He assented. We both stripped to the waist, then I took my knife from its sheath and crept back into the dark chapel. I cut the ankle-bonds of the two captives.

"Work yourselves free, and go home when the tide falls," I said. "If you try to cause any alarm, or leave here before the tide goes down, you die."

Ten minutes later, at the side of de Rohan, I was pushing out our float into the dark waters, with a full realization of how mad and desperate was the venture.

CHAPTER XII

WITH A WOMAN'S HELP, NOTHING IS IMPOSSIBLE

AS my companion had predicted, the water proved very warm, thanks to the league on league of sands—so much warmer than the air that the immersion promised little discomfort. We pushed the float out ahead of us until we were wading waist-deep; then, with a concerted effort, sent it swirling on in advance. We followed swimming until we caught it again, and then settled to our task.

Oddly enough, considering the sort of mad venture on which we were embarked, the first glimpse of those two twinkling lugger-lights had restored all my courage and confidence. It showed, past any doubt, that there was really some sense to the whole absurd game, that Rabaut's apparently harebrained scheme was based upon some solid premises. This acted as a challenge, bidding me gamble against the future with the same firm determination Rabaut himself displayed—bidding me cast aside all cold reckoning and plunge ahead with something of his superb audacity! After all, this match of life and death would go to him who could best juggle the turn of events with each passing moment.

Yet I had need of all my courage as we slowly kicked the float out against the tide, and the dark Mont receded and merged into the night behind, the last touch of earth. Upon us both weighed the oppressive sense of depth below and immensity above, darkness all around us, the horizon doubly black with uncertainty. Fortunately the wind was only a light breeze and the waters but slightly ruffled; although, at the level of the water, all sight of the lugger's lights had vanished, we still had the dark blur of Tombelaine on the right by which to orient our course.

Our progress was of necessity slow, yet it was steady, and we worked easily along in silence. The stars sparkled, yellow diamonds against the blue velvet canopy closing down on every hand. It seemed as though the sky were pressing down upon us as we floated here, infinitesimal human specks on the black gulf. The tiny rippling of our lashed spars was the only sound; insensibly it grew upon us, swelled into a perpetual hissing murmur, a lap-

WITH A WOMAN'S HELP

lapping as of water fingers touching us caressingly and gently, reassuringly, so that fear departed. The same thought was upon us both, for presently de Rohan voiced it.

"God is close in the night, eh? We think of such things in time of doubt—but I like the feel of the water. It's heartening."

I glanced over my shoulder.

"Man is close also," I said grimly. I could see a glimmer of light showing from the base of the Mont. The apparent closeness of it was disconcerting. "Look back! Rabaut is loading the boat, I imagine. Are you tired?"

"Tired? I'm scarcely wet yet!" De Rohan uttered a soft laugh. "Can one be tired when liberty hangs in the balance? No. We're doing excellently."

The quiet steadiness of his voice, so like that of Kerguelec, reassured me. I blessed my luck in lighting upon such a comrade—or was it luck? Was it not, rather, something higher and greater than mere luck—had I not been driving forward to this very meeting, to this very instant of time, from that day in Paris when first I heard of Kerguelec? Perhaps. As de Rohan said, at such a moment we are given to thinking of these things, I prayed no harm might have come to the Breton during this day and evening.

We had slight conception of time; swimming or floating, seconds are magnified into minutes. I think an hour must have passed in this manner, with the flicker of light growing ever more faint behind us. We took it easily, without hurry, for any effort at speed were senseless folly, and we might have need of all our strength before we won through. Our one great peril lay from fog, since we were surely lost if the lightest mist came upon us; imperceptibly, however, the breeze thickened from the direction of the land and we knew this danger was obviated. So we kept on, the whole great bay of Cancale ahead, and behind us the dark masses of the shore, invisible to our limited horizon.

"The lugger, I think," said de Rohan quietly, breaking silence. "Directly to our right, the double twinkle——"

I pulled myself up partially on the float and discerned a faint double star, well to the right.

"Rest," I said, dropping back. "She's away over beyond Tombelaine, and we've plenty of time—she must tack over in this direction."

De Rohan laughed softly, and I demanded the reason.

WITH A WOMAN'S HELP

"Faith, why not laugh?" he returned whimsically. "To think of our incredible madness in setting out like this, hoping to reach the unknown point of contact between that lugger and Rabaut's boat!"

"Think it over then—it's not so mad," I returned. "Rabaut will have two men only, to row a large and heavily laden boat—trust him to take no share in the work! He must go slowly. He must display a light. Also he must take the most direct route possible; therefore he'll come straight out from the Mont and let the lugger come to him. You see?"

De Rohan grunted.

"Aye. You've the right of it, perhaps. Are we far enough out then?"

"Yes."

We relaxed, rested floating, letting the spars hold us up.

Slowly the double twinkle grew plainer and bore down upon us, until beneath it we could make out the black vagueness of sails and hull. The lugger approached us, came so close we could hear the rippling rush of water beside her, the voices on her deck, until we thought she would run us down and made ready to swim for safety. Then she luffed suddenly, with a wild slapping of her dark-brown canvas.

SAINT MICHAEL'S GOLD

"Hold her there!" came a command. "Is that a boat's light?"

"*Oui-da*," rang the assent from aloft.

"Down with the sails."

Ropes squeaked in sheave-blocks, the flapping canvas rattled down, and bare lines of spars were rocking against the stars to the slow swing of the water. The lugger was not thirty feet away from us. De Rohan ducked under the float and came up beside me.

"You want to try and get aboard? We are between her and the shore, so that the boat must pass us closely."

"Do you feel able to swim around her?" I asked. "Unless we find a line, we can't hope to climb up."

He assented. From our position we could see nothing of any boat's light, but the crew of the lugger were setting out a rope ladder, so we knew the time was short. As she lay floating, we were near her stern. I arranged to swim outside and around her, while de Rohan took the inside, and we would meet under her bow. We were in slight danger of being seen, for all hands were intent on the boat or their work.

Without more delay we abandoned our float and struck off. I rounded the stern of the craft, stroking lazily and quietly, scanning her dark sides as I proceeded, but found no sign of any trailing rope. For once, the slovenly French seamanship was not in evidence—we were dealing here with Bretons who knew their business. Presently I caught a voice from the deck above, in a growl.

"This is a queer affair," it said. "I should like to know, me, if our pay is to come in assignats."

"Lucky if we get that much," responded a grumble. "These accursed commissaires are all promises. The *patron* ought to tap this one for an advance—look at the provisions we've stowed! If it were a question of gold, I'd go to China or hell, but why go to the Antilles for pay in worthless paper? We could get a whole cargo of assignats by going to England, where they are given away. Eighteen factories turning them out, eh——"

The voices drifted off as I continued my slow progress. The bows were high, the stubby bowsprit sticking up against the stars, clear of hanging lines. The head of de Rohan came into sight just beyond me. Then I sighted the light of Rabaut's boat.

"No luck," said de Rohan.

"The devil!" I responded softly. "And there's the boat. Where's the ladder put out?"

SAINT MICHAEL'S GOLD

"From the waist."

"Then get back to the stern. Come on around by this side, so we'll not be seen."

We drifted back along the high wall of the lugger until we came to the stern. By this time, the long immersion was telling on us both in a gradual weakening of forces, and I knew de Rohan must be far more drained of strength than I myself. A projection of the rudder afforded a hold, and I indicated it to him.

"Hang on, now, until I come back."

He obeyed. I went on to the other side of the lugger and took stock of things.

The boat was approaching slowly and laboriously. The two grenadiers were making heavy work of it, since this was probably their first encounter with an oar, and the boat was heavy. She was deeply laden, and in the stern a dark mass resolved itself into two figures, and I heard the voice of Rabaut hailing the lugger.

"Hello, there! This is Citizen Commissaire Rabaut. You await me?"

"*Oui-da,* citizen! A ladder is lowered, here by the lantern."

"Good. You have cabins ready?"

WITH A WOMAN'S HELP

"*Diantre!* We are not a frigate, citizen, but we have two cabins. Both are yours."

"Very well. There are two of us, and two soldiers also. Be ready to get my luggage aboard; it is heavy. You are bound for America, on service of the republic; the pay to be in gold. Is it understood?"

"Understood, citizen!" The voice was even joyous. Payment in gold meant much in these days, and meant a hundredfold to thrifty Bretons.

The boat slowly came alongside, and a rope was flung down from above. Pol Rouge, whom I recognized by his hearty curses, caught a crab and went sprawling headlong. Pol Noir got hold of the line but did not know what to do with it. Rabaut scrambled forward, took the line, and ordered him to get hold of the ladder.

I was drifting slowly under the side of the lugger, well beyond the lantern-rays from above. The boat swung in upon me, and with a stroke I was under her stern. Pol Rouge was cursing furiously, Rabaut was snapping orders, while everybody was giving directions above.

"Marie!" I exclaimed under cover of the confusion. "Get out a line from a cabin window—something to climb!"

"Good," she assented. At the same instant Rabaut turned.

"Kerguelec! Come along! Mount, while I hold the ladder."

I dived, lest Rabaut get a glimpse of my head, and struck out for the stern of the lugger.

Exultation thrilled in me, and when I rejoined de Rohan it was with a quick laugh and a blessing for the sharp-witted girl. I told him briefly how I had got word to her, and he uttered a sigh of relief.

"Good enough—I am nearly exhausted. I do not know if I can climb, Martin."

"You will."

We waited an interminable time, or so it seemed, while from the decks resounded tramplings of feet and loud voices. Knowing the two cabins must be in the stern, I had every confidence in Kerguelec's ability to help us from our impasse.

What had been said in my hearing, also, served to clarify the whole situation. Rabaut's powers were supreme, and his orders were obeyed without hesitation; further, his adroit promise of payment in gold had placed ship and crew entirely at his disposition. I had hoped we might look for help from these Bretons, but now it was clear we could expect noth-

ing of the sort—undoubtedly they were rabid revo-
lutionaries and had been chosen for the service by
the local committee in St. Malo to whom Rabaut
had addressed his letter.

A slight noise came from over our heads, then
the voice of Rabaut.

"You'll have this cabin to yourself, I'll take the
other. I must see to the stowage of our cargo,
mademoiselle; if you have need of anything, call a
seaman and demand it. With morning, I'll have
some proper garments for you—I have brought
them with me on purpose. May I have your per-
mission to depart?"

"With pleasure," responded Kerguelec.

I paddled out a stroke or two and looked up. Perhaps eight feet above us showed one lighted stern
window, another to the left being dark. Now, at
the lighted window, appeared head and shoulders,
and the voice of Kerguelec came down.

"You're there?"

"Yes."

"I have no rope!" and the voice was despairing.
"There's nothing—a blanket, perhaps?"

"If you can hold one end of it."

What followed was little less than desperate,
especially as we had no time to waste. Kerguelec

dropped out the blanket, keeping a grip on one corner. In order to get it within my reach, he was forced to lean far out the cabin window, but at length I caught hold. The Breton drew back and managed to get his end across the sill for purchase —-by which time I was out of the water and full weight on the blanket. The climbing was a terrific task, far more difficult than ascending a rope, for only the folds of cloth gave grip to my fingers.

However at length I could reach to the window, and then drew myself up and in, head-first. Kerguelec caught and stayed me as I dropped to the floor and helped me to find my feet.

"All right?"

"All right, thanks." I got out my knife. "The blanket, quickly!"

I seized it and began to slit it into lengths, knotting two of these strips together, for de Rohan could never have come up as I had. Kerguelec at my side breathed a wondering question, and I laughed.

"There's another to come—you'll see!"

I dropped the knotted length of rope until de Rohan, below, caught it. I dragged him up, foot by foot—no easy matter, since he could help himself but little. As last I got his hand in mine, and a final effort brought him up to the window opening.

WITH A WOMAN'S HELP

He poised there, and a gasping word came from him.

"Ha! Your fish is nearly aboard——"

A low cry burst from Kerguelec, who recognized the voice—then de Rohan was in on top of me. I lost balance, and we both went down in a heap. When I struggled up, helping him to his feet, I spoke to Kerguelec. There was no answer—the Breton had fainted. The supreme emotion of finding this brother alive, whom she thought dead, had prevailed.

From this moment, as though it were symbolic, Kerguelec was no more. There remained Marie de Rohan, the woman.

She revived swiftly. For a while brother and sister clung together in tears, she oblivious of his half-naked wetness, her voice melted in soft tenderness, until I wondered anew how she could ever have assumed the man's tones of Kerguelec.

"Ah, Louis, Louis!" and she laughed a little, holding him away to devour his face with her eager gaze. "And they said you were dead—I got messages to some of the priests, bribed a guard to bring me word—fallen, they said, over the cliff!"

"Why did you never tell me of your brother?" I demanded.

257

SAINT MICHAEL'S GOLD

"You are a hard man, Citizen Martin!" She regarded me sideways as she spoke. "You cared for nothing except your own safety—you told me so. You would help me, but not my cause. You were afraid of being dragged into intrigues, you would help no man in particular——"

"Nonsense," I said gruffly, feeling her words all too true. "If you had told me it was a question of your brother—but you tried to bribe me——"

"What, bickering!" de Rohan intervened with a laugh. "Cease, I command it! Friend Martin would never have pulled me alive out of death had he not been a hard man, my sister! I am in his debt, and utterly."

"I also," said the girl, and her hand came out to mine. "Forgive my words—they were not meant in earnest. Besides, it has been hard for me today. Rabaut thinks you dead, and I had small hope of seeing you——"

"Well, better discuss what's to be done," I broke in. "Listen!"

The creaking of sheaves and slatting of canvas apprised us the lugger was getting under way once more. From the stern above us came sounds of a hot argument over the boat. Rabaut had ordered it stove in and abandoned, and this was sacrilege to the thrifty Breton mind. The matter was settled by peremptory commands from Rabaut, and his voice wakened us all to our situation.

In the silence came a heavy step outside, and a hand hammered at the door.

"Well, citizen!" came the voice of Pol Rouge. "Asleep already?"

I hurriedly crowded to one side with de Rohan; the cabin was small and cramped for three of us. Marie took down the lantern from its hook and then opened the door to reveal the mustached Parisian outside with a large bundle.

"Clothes, sent by the citizen commissioner," he said. "Peste! Your cabin floor is most sacredly wet, citizen!"

"It's nothing," said the girl, taking the bundle from him. "I knocked over a pitcher of water. Thank you, citizen."

Pol Rouge stamped away, and the girl closed the door again. She dropped the bundle into one of the two bunks and hung the lantern back on its ceiling hook. De Rohan and I, stripped to the waist, water-soaked, were certainly not very pretty figures, and scarce blamed the girl for smiling as she looked at us.

"Yes, we must decide what to do," she said. "Ra-

259

baut has sent me these woman's garments, and if I wear them——"

She faltered. I caught de Rohan's eye, and both of us were thinking the same thought. A crisis might well impend at any moment; it would depend on how far Rabaut would be in control of his baser self.

"Right." I put the matter frankly. "If the worst comes to the worst, we'll force the issue. Until then, temporize with him! We're forced to depend on Rabaut to a certain extent." I went on to set forth our position. It was certain we could not get out of Cancale Bay without running the gauntlet of the French fleet. "With Rabaut to pull us all through, well and good," I concluded. "Tomorrow morning should tell the tale, I imagine. Given a good breeze, we should be well out of the bay and clear of all danger by tomorrow night."

"Very well," said the girl, and bit her lip. "I'll do my best, I promise you! But—but where ——"

"Where can we stay meantime?" I finished for her. "That's the thing to settle. Perhaps we can get down in the hold, later on——"

The same idea was in all our minds, though neither I nor de Rohan would put it into words.

WITH A WOMAN'S HELP

Under the circumstances, any separation would be rank folly. This cabin was the only safe place for us, and to seek hiding down in the hold, where we might be battened in and lost to all sight or sound of what was passing above, would be an absurdity. Marie looked from one to other of us, and then a smile touched her lips.

"Stay here," she said simply. "There are two berths; one of us must sleep on the floor. It will be only until tomorrow night—you agree?"

I glanced at de Rohan, and he nodded.

"Very well," I assented. "De Rohan, you get into the top bunk yonder. I'll take the floor. Mademoiselle, we'll be asleep in five minutes, by your leave."

And so in fact we were.

CHAPTER XIII

THE little lugger was decidely not a spacious craft, probably having been built for the Holland trade, or for smuggling contraband into England. The two stern cabins opened directly upon a large mess-cabin; this latter also served as saloon, chart room, and lounge. Crew and officers totalled ten, all of them stout Bretons of St. Malo—or more properly termed, Malouins, the finest seamen of France.

These things we learned next morning from Marie. She was gone when I wakened and roused up de Rohan, but returned to bring us bread and wine and news. The lugger was well heeled over and bowling westward under a fresh wind, the day was clear and sunny, and the constant trample of feet on deck bespoke much activity.

The girl stepped in, closed and bolted the door hurriedly, and stood smiling at us. We were a queer-looking pair, unshaven and unwashed, with blankets pulled about our shoulders. I glanced at de Rohan, his lips twitched, and all three of us broke into laughter. Marie still wore her Breton costume, refusing to don the woman's garb until she might have a feeling of greater security in doing so.

"I have one pair of pistols," she observed, as we made way with the bread and wine. "They are in my berth yonder, Monsieur Martin. You'll find your papers and money safely there too."

"Have you seen Rabaut?" I asked, and she nodded assent.

"He's on deck. A ship is in sight—the captain says she's a French frigate, though only a scrap of white is visible."

Here was news! As I had anticipated, it was impossible for any craft to steal out of French waters except by extra good luck. Fearful of an English descent on the coast, anxious to check the continuous enemy communication which was sapping the strength of the republic, a large share of the French navy was concentrated along the western coast on the lookout. As our crew were presumably in service of the republic, they had no reason to try and evade this watch.

SAINT MICHAEL'S GOLD

Marie informed us that the treasure had been chucked below, being carelessly treated by Rabaut as the strongest measure of precaution. Pol Rouge and Pol Noir were seasick at the moment, though no one else aboard was affected. Going to the door, for she was returning on deck at once, the girl paused there and flung her brother a singular glance, whose import when taken with her words was plain enough to us both.

"Rest, both of you," she said. "Get back your strength today—we may have need of it tonight. I'll lock this door, so no one can enter while I'm gone."

She departed. De Rohan looked at me significantly.

"Eh—you comprehend?" he said. "This Rabaut is a beast."

"In this instance beasts prey by night, not by day," I said philosophically, though it was only too easy to understand the peril threatening Marie. "Best do as she says—rest, eat, sleep! If we have come upon a French frigate, we may equally chance upon an English ship, and then show ourselves. That would let the smoke out of Rabaut's balloon in a hurry! However, we can wait and see how Rabaut handles the frigate yonder."

SCRUPLES ARE INJURIOUS—Q. E. D.

Something like an hour afterward came drifting to us the boom of a heavy gun. The lugger promptly came up into the wind, and thus gave us sight, from our stern window, of the frigate. Almost at once an exclamation broke from de Rohan.

"Irony of fate! It's my old ship, the *Bellepoule!* Now we'll see whether he can swing the affair—"

"He can swing the gates of hell off their hinges," I said sourly.

For a little the frigate forged ahead out of our sight, though she came close enough for a hail to be exchanged. The lugger lowered a boat, and as we swung in the wind, we could see the frigate again and the boat heading for her, with Rabaut in the stern. We awaited the upshot with no little anxiety, because our own escape was dependent upon the finesse and audacity displayed by Rabaut.

We soon had proof of his quality. Half an hour elapsed, when his boat left the frigate and started back to us. Almost at once a wreath of white leaped from the side of the frigate, and then gun after gun spoke out. As the heavy reports reached us, we left the window lest Rabaut catch a glimpse of our faces. De Rohan looked at me with a grim smile.

"The rascal! He's made them salute him by way of apology! Well, I suppose they're glad enough

265

to have a chance to burn powder and make a noise—"

So it was, indeed. Before the salute was finished, the boat was aboard and the lugger was heeling over anew to the wind-thrust. In twenty minutes the blue horizon-line of France had sunk out of sight— Rabaut had won his game, we were past the final barrier, and the land was gone. And now—what?

"Excellent!" stated de Rohan. "Now all uncertainty is cleared away, we know what we must face—and I'd give half my fortune for a shave and a bath!"

"You'll get one tonight, or at least the shave," I prophesied. "And perhaps some clothes to boot."

"From the skies?"

"No. From Citizen Rabaut."

He laughed at this, quite comprehending my meaning, and we stretched out to sleep again.

Marie, as she had now become to me, not only from our comradeship but from hearing this name alone on the tongue of her brother, spent most of the afternoon on deck, probably feeling more secure there in the open from any advances on the part of Rabaut.

Twice, in the course of the day, she slipped in to us bearing some food she had managed to secrete—a bottle of wine, some sausage, cheese and bread, rude but nourishing fare. On the second occasion, just after sunset, she came directly from the mess-cabin outside. As she flung back the long hair from her face, after setting down her burden, I saw the look in her eyes and spoke.

"Trouble?"

"Later," she returned laconically.

"Where's Rabaut? Didn't we hear him go into his cabin just now?"

"Yes—don't speak too loudly! He wants me to join him on deck in a few minutes."

"Very good," I said coolly. "Keep him engaged there for a time. Play him carefully. Then tell him to go to his own cabin—intimate that you may receive him here after a little. Remain on deck unless you hear a shot—in that case, watch whether anyone hears or observes it, and let us know."

It was not too nice a part, this, particularly when given a French girl of birth. Her face whitened a little with anger, and her eyes flashed—then, before she could speak, de Rohan intervened gravely.

"This to you, that to us—each one has a task, Marie. Is a little pride more to be regarded than life and liberty?"

Her face softened, and her hand went impulsively to mine.

SAINT MICHAEL'S GOLD

"Of course. I'll do it," she said, and smiled "And it will be well done."

"Where are the two grenadiers—Pol Rouge and Pol Noir?" I asked.

"They are still down with *mal de mer*, I believe. They are forward with the crew. They should be getting over it soon."

"Well, if you take out the lantern, get it refilled and relighted, and then bring it back, we'll not bother you further."

She nodded and departed. All this conversation had been low-voiced, since Rabaut was in his cabin adjoining. Presently she returned with the lighted lantern, and barely had she entered when Rabaut came from his own cabin and knocked at the door.

"I'll be on deck in five minutes," she responded without opening.

"Thank you, mademoiselle," answered Rabaut, and so went his way. I hung up the lantern and spoke softly.

"Tell us whether anyone's in the mess-cabin outside."

She opened the door and pronounced the coast clear. In half a moment de Rohan and I were across in Rabaut's cabin, door closed, lantern on hook.

268

SCRUPLES ARE INJURIOUS—Q. E. D.

Darkness was falling fast. Our first care was to cover over the window with a blanket, lest the reflection of light be caught from the deck above. Then, satisfied of security, we turned to examine the place. One glance showed us that Rabaut, despite his hasty departure from France, had not left any of his personal effects behind. De Rohan broke into a laugh at sight of the clothes—a large portmanteau had been unpacked and the things laid out, so the damp sea air might rid them of wrinkles. Since Rabaut was of large build, his clothes would do me very well.

"Come, Martin! The rogue takes good thought for himself! Here's a case of razors—and what excellent clean linen! Decidedly, we'll appear to good advantage tomorrow, eh?"

De Rohan and I fell to work—keeping, the while, our pistols close at hand. It was not alone vanity and the presence of a woman impelling us to the task of personal adornment, nor even our own desires; but upon this matter might depend the fate of us all, according to the sketchy plans I had formulated.

That two men should long remain hidden aboard this small craft was utterly impossible. The most we could hope for was to remain undiscovered until the morning, and then our one chance was to play a bold game, depending heavily on the impetus of surprise to aid us. At best, we were two against a dozen, and must count on moral force rather than any mere physical prowess. Rabaut once disposed of, my chief fears lay with Pol Rouge and Pol Noir. Those two stupid, earnest, courage-blinded Parisian grenadiers were anything but negligible. Also I was aware, but not sufficiently aware, that man proposes and God disposes.

Half an hour or more passed. Shaved and bathed, we were like new men, particularly de Rohan. Thus emerging, his features showed the same delicate strength as those of his sister, though he was much her senior. Food and wine had combined to bring some color into his cheeks and rid him of weakness, and I knew he could be depended on heavily.

Once shaved and cleansed, we turned to Rabaut's supply of fine apparel, and took delight in sharing his finery. There was enough of it to equip us both, from stock to breeches, and de Rohan drew to his share a pair of diamond-buckled shoes—but there I was at a loss. Not being built on French lines, footgear was a problem; barefoot I came into this lugger, and barefoot I would remain aboard her, it seemed.

SCRUPLES ARE INJURIOUS—Q. E. D.

Without a warning came a sharp rap at the door and the voice of Marie.

"Coming!"

She passed on without pause. I caught up my pistol when de Rohan, cocking his own weapon, laid a hand on my arm.

"My friend, remember the debt I owe this man," he said earnestly. "He sent my brother to death and me to prison. Leave him to me, I beg of you! That pistol-shot must come from my hand."

"Conceded and gladly," I said, with a shrug. "But Marie has not obeyed—she should have gone on deck—"

"There was some reason. Perhaps she thought best to warn us. Then the man is mine?"

I nodded and sat down in the lower bunk. We did not have long to wait. The lugger was heeling over slightly, groaning and protesting in every timber, and we did not hear Rabaut's approach until he was at the door and his voice sharply exclaiming.

"A light! But who—"

He flung open the door, swinging it back against the bunks. Thus he did not see me at all, but stepped into the cabin to find himself face to face with Louis de Rohan. Pistol in hand, the latter smiled.

SAINT MICHAEL'S GOLD

"Welcome, M. le Marquis! I've been waiting for you."

Never have I seen a man so absolutely stupefied as Rabaut in this moment—and he of all men! Here on this ship, far out at sea, when all difficulties were passed and he had brought his affair to a triumphant conclusion—a dead man appeared before him. More, a man whom he had betrayed to death! Small wonder his normal coolness deserted him, and his cynical disbelief in anything was staggered, and the possibility of the supernatural surged upon him in a tremendous wave.

He put out a hand to the wall, as though groping for the feel of something solid. I kicked the door, so it slammed shut to a swing of the ship, but he never looked at me, never knew I was there. His usually keen eyes became large and protruding, fastened upon de Rohan in a fixed stare. The color ebbed out of his face.

"Louis!" he exclaimed huskily. He must have known de Rohan well in other days. "Louis! No, no—you're dead—"

"Certainly, and I've come back for you," said de Rohan quietly. "My brother Charles sent me. You remember him? And others sent me, too. Baron Nissen, whom you gave to the mob at Versailles.

SCRUPLES ARE INJURIOUS—Q. E. D.

De Rochefort, whom you betrayed to Marat while he was at your dinner table. Fleurus, who—"

"Stop!" cried out Rabaut, struggling for self-control, for comprehension. "This is past belief—you couldn't be here—"

"No? But I am here, St.-Servaut! Perhaps the prayers of my sister have brought me—had this occurred to you as a possibility? And I am about to kill you."

Rabaut's two pistols lay in the upper berth, yet he made no move toward them. He could not drag his eyes from de Rohan, and now it seemed I had woefully misjudged the man's ability in a pinch. With one hand he fumbled in mechanical fashion at his waistcoat, as though unable to get out his snuff-box. With the other he supported himself against the wall, for the lugger was beginning to lurch badly. He wet his lips, tried to speak and could not. He was a pitiful spectre of himself.

De Rohan, merciless, now sent in a deadly thrust. It must have astounded Rabaut beyond measure.

"To top all else, traitor, you have not hesitated to steal the gold belonging to St. Michael himself, eh? That reached you, did it? No, M. le Marquis, there's nothing I don't know—nothing! Do you really expect that St. Michael will let you get away with all this treasure of his?"

Upon these words, de Rohan swung up his pistol. Rabaut flinched visibly, his deathly white face streaming with cold sweat.

"Stop!" he exclaimed. "Stop! I'll make reparation—"

"Reparation—from you?" de Rohan's laugh was bitter with scorn. "Reparation for blood and treachery? Dog that you are—"

"Wait, wait!" broke out Rabaut. He took an unsteady step forward. "Give me time—you cannot shoot me down like this—*arrah!*

Swift as light, a growl on his lips, he hurled himself forward.

Of all things, such a move on his part was most unexpected. He had placed himself craftily, timing his spring to a thrust of the deck, balancing himself perfectly. So tigerish was his leap, he actually knocked the pistol out of de Rohan's hand before the latter could pull trigger, and the weapon fell without exploding.

Flashing up from his waistcoat pocket, Rabaut's left hand showed a small spring-knife, the blade open. De Rohan was knocked backward against the muffled window. One cry burst from him as

SCRUPLES ARE INJURIOUS—Q. E. D.

Rabaut's knife plunged; then he went down, falling on the deck. Rabaut was over him instantly, gripping back his head with one hand, thrusting again with the knife for the bared throat.

Rabaut was plunging home the knife when I shot him.

It was a quick, hasty shot—the rapidity of his attack had found me entirely unprepared. He pitched sidelong, the blade dropping from his hand, and then rolled in a limp heap against the side wall. I scrambled out of my bunk, threw aside the pistol, and rushed to help de Rohan, who was feebly trying to pull himself up. He came to one elbow, caught my hand, and sat up.

"The rogue—outwitted me!" he said faintly. "My side—"

I saw how he was hurt. The little knife had gashed into his side below the ribs; a deep and nasty cut, bleeding profusely. Scarcely had I laid bare the hurt, when a rattle at the door brought me erect, as Marie stepped into the cabin.

She stood motionless an instant, taking in everything at a glance. Words were needless. What had happened was plain to see.

"Something for a bandage, and swiftly," I said.

She nodded and disappeared. I stooped and helped de Rohan to his feet.

"Arm around my neck—that's right! We'll get into our own cabin and then fix you up—careful, now!"

We had only a few steps to go. The mess cabin was empty, and another lantern was swinging in Marie's cabin. She met us, some garment torn into strips for bandages, and helped me lower her brother into the under berth, then brought water. In a moment I was washing and binding up the wound. De Rohan was unconscious by this time, chiefly from loss of blood, for the hurt itself was not mortal by a good deal.

"Was the shot heard on deck?" I demanded, as I worked.

"Yes, but it was muffled, and no one was sure about it. What happened?"

"Rabaut was too clever," I returned. "Your brother should have shot first and talked afterward. Keep an eye out, will you, in case anyone comes?"

She left the cabin. Another five minutes and I had finished the job, and a good job it was. There seemed little reason why de Rohan should not be on his feet by morning, with care. I went outside and almost collided with Marie in the darkness.

SCRUPLES ARE INJURIOUS—Q. E. D.

"All clear," she said. "Is Rabaut—dead?"

"I hope so devoutly," I answered. "Haven't had time yet to make sure. Your brother's all right, Marie. Look after him tonight—sleep is his best remedy. In the morning put on your woman's clothes. We'll have to make a strong play to get control of this lugger, and it must be done first thing. Good night!"

"Good night," she said in a low and singular voice.

"Eh? What it is, comrade?" I asked. "Have I offended you?"

"No, no!" she returned, with swift breaths. "No! I don't see how—how you can keep on fighting against everything—with Louis gone—"

I laughed and patted her hand, and her fingers clung to mine.

"Nonsense! Who else could fight for you—and who wouldn't fight for you? Everything's all right. Good night again."

This time her response was more natural. "And God keep you!" she added.

I went back into Rabaut's cabin and closed the door.

When I leaned over the body of Rabaut, a terrible temptation grew upon me. He was not dead, by

277

evil chance. My bullet had cut across his scalp over the ear—he was not even hurt to any extent. What I should do was plain enough.

To open the window and shove out his unconscious figure would be the work of a moment. He would have a swift and merciful death, far better than he deserved. Otherwise he would only have to be killed in worse fashion. To think of leaving him alive, even in bonds, was impossible. It would be the veriest folly to hold him prisoner on such a voyage as this—he had just proved his ability full measure!

Hesitate over it? Yes, and for a long moment. For all our sakes, the thing cried out to be done. It was common sense. And as I hesitated, came a tap on the door, and it opened to let Marie enter.

"Again," she said, closing the door and regarding me. "I felt I had to know—about him. He's not dead?"

"Unfortunately, no," I said bitterly. "My bullet only scraped his head."

"Then—"

I met her gaze, read her alarm, her unuttered question, and smiled sourly.

"You called me a hard man, eh? Well, perhaps I am. This rascal must be killed, if we are to live.

SCRUPLES ARE INJURIOUS—Q. E. D.

He deserves it. He has earned death a hundred times over. Is it not so?"

"Yes," she said, steadily watching me.

"Well, there is the window, there is a pistol, there is his own knife," I indicated the various means of disposal. "Which shall it be?"

She glanced at the sprawled, unconscious figure and then back at me.

"Eh? You mean—"

"Kill him if you wish," I said, and shrugged. "I'm no murderer. If we can carry the game through in the morning, I'll have him hung. There'd be a sense of justice to that, eh? But to let the life out of a helpless man is the act of a rank coward. I wish I could do it, but it's out of the question for me."

She smiled suddenly.

"Good night again, monsieur!" she said, and quietly departed, leaving me to a puzzled wonder.

So I bound Rabaut hand and foot, gagged him, and went to bed.

CHAPTER XIV

THE BATTLE IS NOT TO THE WEAK

I WAKENED to find the level rays of earliest sunlight flooding in at the stern window, though it promised to be gone soon enough. The wind was so light, the lugger was almost on an even keel, and off to the south were banked tremendous black clouds, promising some heavy weather ere long.

I dressed, paying no heed to Rabaut, who lay glaring at me, wide awake. My first care was to take stock of defences. With the two pistols from Marie, and Rabaut's weapons, we were fairly well armed, so I loaded and primed them and laid them ready. Then I removed the gag from Rabaut's mouth, gave him a drink, and propped him up in the corner of the cabin. I sat on the edge of the bunk and regarded him appraisingly.

His lips were still too swollen for ready speech, and the bonds must have caused him no little pain— not to mention his untended wound, whence a trickle of blood had dried over his cheek.

THE BATTLE IS NOT TO THE WEAK

"This is a very pleasant little surprise for you, eh?" I said cheerfully, mocking his little trick of speech. "A clever trick of yours, friend Rabaut, to arrange my disposal at the Mont—eh? Well, treachery is a good game temporarily, not as a permanent thing. Your jug has gone to the well once too often, and now you'll hang for your sins, I trust. You failed to kill de Rohan last night, and I failed to kill you, but a length of rope will soon set the matter right. You may shout if you like—and I'll put a bullet into you."

He made no pretense of astonishment or any other emotion. There was no way he could trick me now, and he knew it.

"I've procured your escape," he said thickly.

I laughed at this, and as I laughed the venom in his eyes grew deeper.

"Don't be silly," I said, and sobered. "I'm procuring my own escape, thank you. It's a pity de Rohan didn't pistol you last night; somewhere, there's a reason of destiny in that. I rather believe in destiny, Rabaut, or in the adage that all's for the best if one regards it aright! You might not agree with me at the moment, I concede. Well, perhaps your life was spared in order to let me learn from you—eh? Come! Would sparing you be of advantage to us or to anyone else? Can you set out any reason why you shouldn't hang?"

"The gold," he muttered, staring at me, too hopeless even to gather his faculties and make a bid for life.

"What gold? You have none. All aboard here is mine if I want it—though I don't. I'm no thief. Perhaps you have some papers or information of value?"

He made a frantic clutch at the straw of hope.

"Yes. There's a French squadron ahead of us. I can get you past safely—"

"On this ocean? Bah! None of your lies. It won't do, my friend! Since you've nothing worth while to offer, back goes the gag."

He cursed me most horribly, but I suited action to words and replaced the gag, at the risk of bitten fingers. I appropriated his pistol-sash, buckled it around me, and put two pistols in the pockets, then took the others in hand and opened the door. Peering out, I found the mess-cabin empty, and crossed quickly to that of Marie. At my knock, she opened the door and I stepped in.

"Ready? Ah! My salutations, mademoiselle— and heartiest congratulations!"

To tell the truth, she astonished me beyond words,

THE BATTLE IS NOT TO THE WEAK

this being my first sight of the real Marie de Rohan. Gone was Kerguelec, boots, breeches and black hat. The long Breton hair was now pinned up, she wore a very handsome, if not new, gown of blue flowered silk, and a kerchief was pinned about her throat. Where the magic had come from I could not say, but every touch of the dark Kerguelec had vanished, and here before me stood a smiling, bright-eyed girl, a perfect stranger, greeting my surprised regard with a gay courtsey.

"Ha, Martin!" cried de Rohan from his berth. "What news?"

I turned to him. "We go to make news, I trust. How are you?"

"Well enough. No fever at all events. Marie won't let me up, though I'm able—"

"Then get up," and I held out my hand to his.

He came to his feet, staggered a little, then quickly steadied. Marie intervened with anxious protest.

"But, Monsieur Martin, he is not able to exert himself!"

"He must become able, then," I said, and glanced at some bread and wine she must have procured before my arrival. "Something to eat and drink— good! We'll have need of every ounce of help we can get. You go on deck, now, and wait near the companionway until we come up. It won't be long."

She obeyed, after one slightly rebellious look which I disregarded. So long as de Rohan could walk, he would serve my purpose, since we were in no shape to take into consideration anything except the pressing need of all three.

I helped him to finish dressing, as he was already partially clothed, and then we divided the wine and bread. I gave him the two extra pistols, and we were ready.

"You'll have to grin and bear it," I said. "No one will suspect your condition. Get an arm around my neck—"

"No, I can manage all right with your arm to lean on," he intervened.

We left the cabin together, and I told him about Rabaut's present condition. The deck-ladder came down directly into the mess-cabin, and as we reached it, I realized this was actually my first appearance on board, my first sight of the lugger beyond the stern-cabins. Well, it was likewise the lugger's first sight of me, and I was counting heavily on the effect of surprise. By this time, the crew must all be gawking at Marie, whom they certainly would never recognize for Kerguelec.

THE BATTLE IS NOT TO THE WEAK

We slowly mounted, de Rohan leaning on me, and as we neared the deck paused.

"Go ahead, Martin. I'll make my appearance after you. Pity I didn't shoot that rascal last night! I owe you my life again. Go ahead."

I went on and came up through the open hatch to the deck.

Marie was standing a little aft of me, by the rail. Three men stood by the wheel, staring at her. Forward, the crew were gathering, all eyes for this stupefying apparition of a woman. The cook, serving out some soup from a kettle, paused with the others and was gaping aft, his mouth wide open. All these men were rough Malouins, either fishermen or smugglers by profession, with little distinction between the crew and officers. Pol Rouge and Pol Noir were just coming on deck forward.

My appearance created a new sensation. The three men aft hurriedly crossed themselves as I approached Marie—a significant gesture. The two grenadiers, catching sight of me, stopped short, incredulous.

"Give your brother a hand," I said to the girl, and then turned toward the three men by the wheel. These looked hard at me, shrank slightly from my approach, and nodded a reply to my greeting.

285

SAINT MICHAEL'S GOLD

"Good day! Which of you is the captain?"

"C'est moi," said one, a burly, heavily bearded seaman with a red cap. "I am the patron, monsieur ——"

"Will you be good enough to call your men together here? I've something to say to all of you."

"But where are you from? Where's Citizen Rabaut?" demanded the skipper.

"You'll learn in a moment, my friend."

The skipper bawled at his men, and then broke off to stare at de Rohan, who was now appearing.

"Name of the devil!" he cried out sharply. "Where are you all coming from? How many more of you down below? Where's that lanky rascal of a Breton?"

"He's dead," I said curtly. This was enough to bring them all up with a round jerk.

The men came lurching aft, all staring hard, and the two grenadiers followed. De Rohan joined Marie at the rail. He leaned easily against it, with no sign of his real weakness except his pallor. I drew out both pistols as though to examine the priming, and the advancing men promptly halted. I said nothing. Silence and significant actions were for the moment my best allies.

As I had descried on first waking, the sunlight

THE BATTLE IS NOT TO THE WEAK

was already doomed and failing fast. The whole sky to the south was now a mass of black cloud, rapidly reaching across the zenith and swallowing up all the dayspring. The wind had faded out to a mere breath, so that the canvas flapped half idly; the ocean had become a rolling, glassy mass of gray water. Here was one of those slow-gathering, slow-breaking storms, and it might hold off an hour or half a day—though it would be a bad one when it broke.

Now occurred a tiny thing—tiny, for the weight of destiny hanging upon it later. The helmsman touched Redcap's arm and pointed off to the north. Following the gesture, I discerned a fleck of white, a scrap of sail against the horizon. Redcap drew a telescope from his pocket and unfolded it, looked at the sail, then slammed the glass shut with a shrug.

"Nothing," he said. "A small craft."

He turned toward me with obvious intent to speak, but I forestalled him in the effort to get control of the situation.

"Pol Rouge! Pol Noir! Step out here."

The two hairy rascals left the clumped mass of men, both of them still in dumbfounded amazement at my appearance.

"You know me," I said curtly. "You, Pol

SAINT MICHAEL'S GOLD

Rouge! Tell these honest seaman my name and position."

Pol Rouge growled. "Citizen Martin, assistant commissioner of the Paris committee—or so called. Citizen Rabaut has given orders to arrest you, as being nothing of the sort."

"A lie," I stated. Putting up one pistol, I felt in my pocket, fortunately having taken my papers and money from Marie. I drew out the commission and handed it to the skipper. "Read for yourself, citizen."

He handled it gingerly, spelled out the words, and nodded.

"Right," he commented, to the stupefaction of the two grenadiers. I addressed them promptly, hoping to advantage myself by whatever lies Rabaut had told them—perhaps he had simply told them the truth about me.

"You two worthy soldiers of the republic have been made the dupe of a rascal," I said. "You have aided Citizen Rabaut to steal a lot of valuables, the property of the state. You have aided him to embark them by night aboard this lugger for America. Is there any reason why you should not be tried and hung for the crime?"

"Eh? Eh?" stammered Pol Rouge, over the

288

THE BATTLE IS NOT TO THE WEAK

spokesman for the pair. "What's all this about, citizen? Why, Citizen Rabaut is acting under direct orders from Paris—he has been ordered to America ——"

"Nothing of the sort," I interrupted. "He was sent to Mont St. Michel to bring those things back to Paris. You yourselves know he gave orders to confine me there, in order that he might escape with his plunder. If acting by orders, would he not have gone to St. Malo and there embarked, or Brest? Aye! He would have gone on a frigate, not on a little lugger. Well, I have put Rabaut under arrest. Now, citizen soldiers, it may be you have acted innocently in this matter. If so, here's your chance to speak."

The two grenadiers looked at each other, then at me, in a mingling of perplexity and wrath. Instantly I could see my words had failed to penetrate their stupidly stubborn heads. No reason could overawe them. Instead of trying to sway these two, I should have won over the crew—perhaps it was not too late yet!

"Citizen Rabaut promised you pay in gold," I said, turning to Redcap. "Well, you shall have your pay in gold from me as well, if you want it. Hold

289

your course for America. Citizen Rabaut is to be hanged. Are you satisfied?"

There was a growl of dissent. The skipper pushed back his cap, scratched his grizzled head, and looked from me to Marie and de Rohan.

"Gold is gold, aye," he said. "Still, citizen, there's no proof of your tale. For all I know to the contrary, Citizen Rabaut may be the honest man and you the rascal, trying to make away with his effects! Once you hang him, his mouth is stopped. Let's have him up here and argue it out."

"Not a bit of it," I said promptly. "Come! An oath is an oath. If I and my friends here will take oath on the cross that my——"

The skipper flamed up at me angrily. He and the others might be ardent republicans, but being Bretons, were far from abjuring their faith; and now it seemed I had gone about things in the wrong way, had committed myself to the wrong cause, to win them over.

"What's an oath to you or any other fine Parisian?" he growled out. "May the little black man fly away with the lot of you! A pack of murdering rascals, that's what you and your committee are! What regard have you for sacred things?"

"Regard enough," I cried out, to quell the swift

THE BATTLE IS NOT TO THE WEAK

mutter echoing his words. "Where's all the luggage Rabaut brought aboard? Get it out and look at it. You'll find he has plundered sacred places—Mont St. Michel itself! Get it out and look! It'll show you quickly enough what sort of man he is."

This gripped and held all of them aghast—the Malouins, because of their superstition and reverence for the sacred Mont, the two grenadiers, in sheer dismay. What tale Rabaut had told these two to account for taking the gold, I never learned, yet it must have been a cunning story and far from the truth.

"Break out one of those leathern sacks!" bawled Redcap at his men. "We'll soon see about this tale!"

Two of the men went leaping forward and fell to work on the hatch there. The others muttered among themselves. Pol Rouge and Pol Noir put their heads together. I turned to de Rohan.

"If you have to shoot, don't waste your bullets! Mademoiselle, at the first sign of trouble, get below."

"You're afraid of the outcome?" she asked quietly.

"It's touch and go—anything is possible," I

returned. "Somehow I've failed to hit the right note——"

"They are independent, these Malouins," she said, with a glance at the men up the deck. "They don't take dictation easily—ah! Pol Rouge wants you."

"Citizen Martin!" The big grenadier took a step toward us. "If this is as you say, then we have acted innocently. But how do we know? Perhaps, as this seaman says, you are the rogue and Citizen Rabaut the honest man. After all, he is the commissioner, you are only his assistant! This is a matter to be talked over in due form——"

"Shut your mouth," I ordered abruptly. "This is a matter in which you take orders from me, or else a bullet. Stand back."

He glared at me, and over his shoulder, Pol Noir. They had cooked up some fine scheme, these two ruffians, yet my entire readiness to press trigger was disconcerting and held them hesitant. At this moment too came intervention from another source, as a shout rang out from the forward deck.

The two men there were coming aft, dragging along the planks one of the leather sacks. The others surrounded them, and knives flashed. In an instant the leather was ripped apart. From the rent

THE BATTLE IS NOT TO THE WEAK

sack fell out some of Rabaut's choicest pickings—
several gold chalices, a magnificent gem-studded
ciborium, and among other objects the wondrous
pastoral cross of ancient silver-work.

Now fell a long hush all up and down the deck.
Men crossed themselves and stared wide-eyed at the
unbelieveable plunder, yet said no word; superstition was deeply rooted in these seamen and they
were frightened by what they beheld. Then, abruptly, one glanced up and around, then others.

It was not mere fancy that a deeper and more
terrible hush had descended upon the sea. The
breeze was gone flat away, and the clouds had rolled
up across the sun, though the heat of the morning
was not lessened. In this stillness, the brown canvas flapped and tugged a little, then hung listless.
Unexpectedly a seaman's voice added a touch of awe
to the silence, ringing loudly.

"Punishment! The curse of sacrilege is upon
us all!"

As though stung by these words, the skipper
seized his red cap and flung it to the deck, in an
access of passionate dismay.

"Dogs of destroyers, all of you!" he screamed
out furiously. "One as bad as another—all you
Parisians are alike, destroyers of churches and

293

murderers of priests! All of you Blues are guilty
wretches——"

There, in a flash, his words showed me where I
had missed the great point of appeal, in not stat-
ing instantly who we were. He and the others
thought us no better than Rabaut, when the mere
name of de Rohan might have effected wonders.
Fool that I was! However, it was not too late. I
realized now what card to play, and saw the whole
game won by playing it. Then, as I opened my
lips to speak, came a low groan from behind me.

I glanced around, to see de Rohan staggering.
Perhaps his efforts had disarranged the bandage,
perhaps it was a mere sudden swirl of weakness.
Deathly pale, he reeled and caught at the rail; the
pistols escaped from his hands to fall clattering on
the deck, not exploding. He drooped forward, and
Marie caught him in her arms.

"At them!"

De Rohan's fall was the signal—with one short,
fierce yell, they were in upon me. The two grenadiers were foremost, the seamen followed with a
burst of imprecations. De Rohan struggled to lift
himself.

"I am Louis de Rohan!" he cried faintly. "This
is my sister——"

THE BATTLE IS NOT TO THE WEAK

Too late! The name reached some of them, but failed to check the rush, and his words were drowned in the roar of my pistol.

My first bullet took Pol Rouge fair between the eyes. His body crashed forward and struck me across the legs, sweeping my feet from under me. The shock caused my second bullet to miss Pol Noir, but took life from the skipper, whirled him around, dropped him. Then Pol Noir was on top of me, snarling, a furious beast.

We went rolling across the deck, while all around us volleyed up a medley of shouts and oaths and wild words. Half the seamen were at me, the others trying to haul them off, while Marie could only cower against the rail and support her senseless brother. Next moment I beat Pol Noir from my throat, wrenched clear of his clutching hands, and gained my feet. Using the heavy pistol as a club, I swung as he came for me, and swung again. The two blows brained him, left him in a huddled heap.

"Stop this madness!" I struck another man down, leaped clear, tried to regain what I had lost. "I am an American—here are two of your own de Rohans, Bretons like you——"

A belaying-pin, flung from behind, smashed me

across the back of the head. I swayed dizzily, staggering under the blow. Instantly two of them were upon me, had me by the throat, were throttling me against the rail. Across the blackened sky ripped a flash of lightning, and in the wild glare of it I glimpsed a terrible thing.

From the companionway was emerging the figure of Rabaut, dragging himself slowly and painfully, still nearly numb—somehow he had rid himself of bonds and gag, perhaps by means of his little spring-knife forgotten on the cabin floor. Sight of him was paralyzing. I saw Marie pick up one of her brother's fallen pistols and pull trigger point-blank at Rabaut—it missed fire, the priming gone.

Then Rabaut's voice reached me faintly, and nothing else. The two seamen rammed my skull into the bulwark and I was knocked senseless. And so we lost the game, almost at the moment of success.

CHAPTER XV

A S the voice of Rabaut had been my last memory, so it was my first recognition upon wakening.

Probably I had been unconscious no great length of time—ten minutes at the outside—for when I opened my eyes, my head was still ringing with the two cracks I had received, and the scene was little changed. The ship was still hanging listlessly in the breathless heat and growing darkness, while the sea moved in a long, slow swell that rocked spars and canvas against the blackening sky.

I was bound hand and foot and laid against the starboard rail. Pol Rouge and his brother were both dead, and the Malouin skipper was coughing away his life near the wheel. Half across the deck from me, by the foot of the after mast, sat Marie. In her lap she held the head of her brother, and was leaning over working at his bandages. He, poor fellow, was still unconscious. Near them, fully master of the situation, stood Rabaut.

He had just finished some sort of harangue to the seamen. Whatever he said, the crafty scoundrel had swung events to suit his own purposes—the Malouins, flung into consternation by the death of their master, accepted Rabaut's dominance without protest. He must have rattled off some most remarkable story, for Marie was glancing up at him wide-eyed as though herself wondering at his tale. Her face startled me, it was so thin-drawn, so set in desperate lines, so past all hope.

Rabaut turned to me and met my eyes. He was rubbing away at his wrists, his hair was matted and his cheek blackened with his own dried blood, and yet in this moment he seemed perfectly himself—bitterly cruel of eye, with his same cynical and debonair manner. He was about to speak, when a thunderbolt split heaven and sea asunder with deafening crepitation, blinding us all momentarily. The very ship beneath us quivered and rocked to that electric blast.

When I could see him again, Rabaut was feeling for his snuffbox.

"Decidedly a storm is at hand—eh?" he observed calmly. "Well, Citizen Martin, you have changed your mind about hanging me, perhaps? You'll very soon be stretching a rope yourself—at the present moment, I've more important business on hand. You men there! Tie up that bag of gold and chuck it below, and then make the hatches fast—make everything fast! Get this canvas down, you fools! Do you want to be sunk like a shot when the storm breaks on us? Move, blast you!"

Always audacious, spendthrift of his personality, he lashed them with bitter oaths and sharp orders, and the men obeyed him without protest. Some fell to work about the hatch up forward, after the gold had been bundled together and thrown below, and others went at the sails.

Rabaut stamped forward among them, taking very efficient charge of things—he was all virile energy, in decided contrast with the seamen. Perhaps the heavy, oppressive atmosphere had affected them, for they appeared only half alive, fearful, expectant of they knew not what, and yielded dumbly. Rabaut seemed to have a good deal of ship-knowledge, and had taken hold at an opportune moment. His luck, obviously, held good.

It was not all luck, however. I lay silent, feeling words needless and futile; I was robbed of leadership, of triumph, of everything, by this man. Sight of his bleeding wrists, as he came back toward the stern, showed my conjecture as to his escape had been correct. If luck helped him, it was because he helped himself first.

"So we still head for America together—eh?" He halted before Marie, and surveyed her with his thin grimace of a smile. "And shall I hang this brother of yours at the same time honest Citizen Martin swings? Speak quickly! Bid me for his life, if you want it—what price, eh? When the canvas is down, the corpses go up!"

Marie made no answer, but stared up as though she had not heard the words, and Rabaut turned away with a shrug.

How long the storm would hold off was a question, but the Malouins had wakened to their peril and were at work with a will getting in the canvas. One among them was undoubtedly the mate of the lugger, for his authority over the others appeared unquestioned.

The heavens were by this time solidly overcast with high black clouds, and a breeze was coming up from the south-east, though still a very slight breath of air. Lightning zigzagged across the horizon, and whether or not we were in the storm center, everything was motionless and ominously quiet, heavy with suspense. Only a rag or two of sail left forward, the lugger still swayed to the slow, even swell.

Rabaut had picked up the two pistols dropped by de Rohan and Marie. From his pocket he now produced a very handsome little silver flask, and primed the weapons. He laid them on a water-butt lashed to the rail and turned as three of the men approached him—the mate leading them.

"What's the meaning of all this, citizen?" demanded the mate abruptly, coming face to face with Rabaut and wearing an air of determination. "If this gold of yours is stolen from the sacred Mont, we want to know about it."

Without a word, Rabaut calmly reached over to the water-butt, took up one of the pistols with a negligent air—and shot the man through the head.

A cry of horror burst from Marie. However, with a sense of detachment, I could not deny a certain admiration for Rabaut. This man knew exactly what to do and say, did it and said it, all swiftly and without an instant's hesitation. It shamed me bitterly, when compared with the bungling way I had handled things this morning.

"This way, citizen seamen!" he called, his penetrating voice reaching all of the men alow and aloft.

SAINT MICHAEL'S GOLD

Most of them were already coming on the run. The second pistol in hand, Rabaut faced them coolly. "Question me, and you die. Obey my orders, and you live. None other can save you, now! Think twice about it—eh?"

His indomitable coolness, the stark courage gleaming in those piercing eyes of his, the insolent dominance of his manner, drove home the terrific truth of all he said—as did the still twitching body at his feet. The men halted, crossed themselves, stared, yielded to him in terrified silence.

"Go make ready a line," and Rabaut jerked the long pistol toward two of them. "We'll hang the fool who has caused all this trouble."

The two men obeyed. Rabaut uncocked his pistol, ordered the other men to remove the bodies, and turned to Marie.

"Well, mademioselle, it's time to have an answer. Shall I spare your brother or not—eh? What do you bid?"

"Do as you like, you traitor," she said, and lowered de Rohan's head to the deck. Then she stood up and faced Rabaut. "Do you think I would stoop to beg so low a creature as you for anything?"

The quiet scorn of her manner drew a grimace to his features.

302

NOT EVEN SAINT MICHAEL

"You'll beg soon enough," he said ominously, and motioned a pair of the men who were about lifting Redcap's body. "Here you! Come and hold her."

The men turned and came forward, though uneasily enough. Marie flashed one look that halted them, and her voice leaped out.

"Lay hands on a de Rohan—you men of Bretagne?"

"Eh?" One of the men scratched his head, staring. "Is this true, eh? The de Rohans are princes and good Christians——"

"You might better obey them," said the girl, "than the orders of this man who plunders churches and holy places!"

They shrank a little, but Rabaut laughed.

"Come, come, mademoiselle!" he exclaimed lightly. "Don't force matters to extremes, I beg you! As a matter of fact, I'm tempted to spare our good Louis, since I may have need of him. He's a much better seaman than I, and to reach America——"

"You'll never reach America!" cried out the girl. "Never!"

So strong was her voice, so confident her manner, even Rabaut gave her a swift, keenly startled look, and all the men stared. She jerked at her neck and drew forth the same little rosary of wood which once had so nearly exposed Kerguelec. Others of the men came around, drawn by the scene.

"What do you mean?" demanded Rabaut, frowning at her.

"Blasphemer!" she cried. "You dream of reaching America with the sacred treasure stolen from Mont St. Michel—with blood of murdered men on your hands—fool that you are! Do you imagine there is no such thing as the vengeance of heaven? The very gold you have stolen from the sacred altars will bring its own punishment."

I think Rabaut believed her suddenly gone out of her head. So, to tell the truth, did I, for in all frankness I did not repose any too great confidence in the idea of direct punishment from heaven for sacrilege or anything else. In my experience the vengeance of heaven works through slow natural causes—any direct interposition is too petty a thing for so vast a force.

Yet, as Marie stood shaking the wooden cross at Rabaut, she was transfigured with a furious earnestness, and the passionate conviction of her voice and air was almost frenzied. Perhaps it was only the utterance of her own hopelessness.

NOT EVEN SAINT MICHAEL

"Do you think your violence and treachery can go on for ever?" she cried. "No! Whose were the lives you have destroyed—your own or God's? Whose is this very gold you have thieved—this gold for which you have betrayed yourself doubly and trebly? It belongs to the Prince of Heaven, to the archangel Michael himself; it is from him you have stolen, not from the petty hands of men! Back from him, you men of Bretagne—back from this traitor whose whole existence makes a mock of God and man!"

At these wild words Rabaut himself drew away from the girl, uneasily. As he backed toward the men, they in turn fell away from him. All the deep superstition of their nature was aroused, and among their mutterings I caught repeated the name of de Rohan. Rabaut caught this also, and it stung him.

"You are raving, girl!" he said in contempt, none too well assumed. "What do you prophesy—eh? That St. Michael, in whom you seem so fervently to believe, will descend from heaven to reclaim this gold of his?"

She stood for a moment regarding him, and I perceived that the frenetic outburst had exhausted her. As though broken by his jeering mockery, she turned suddenly and sank into a crumpled heap beside her brother. For a moment her straining, agonized gaze went to me, and in those eyes I could read her deep and terrible despair. Then she flung herself down across de Rohan's body with long, gasping sobs.

"Bah!" Rabaut fumbled out his snuffbox. "Here, two of you! Get this former assistant commissioner up to the halter——"

A tremendous flare, a rending, deafening bolt interrupted him—the lightning must have struck the water close beside us. In the darkness following startled oaths of terror went up from the Malouins. Another flash, this time high across the sky, showed me Rabaut standing there transfixed, unopened snuffbox in hand, looking upward. Then the very heavens opened in blinding fury.

Describe the thing I cannot. One instant was a frightful, intolerable glare of light, a shock of sound splitting the ears, a horrible sense of doom beyond human suffrance; the ship beneath us heaved and splintered. The whole figure of Rabaut was bathed in a whitish radiance; he toppled forward and vanished. Everything vanished, lost in a dense blackness. The bolt had struck us—or had St. Michael smitten down Rabaut in this appalling moment?

Slowly grew the darkened daylight once more, as

NOT EVEN SAINT MICHAEL

the dazzle passed away, with a smell of burning. Half stupefied, I found myself still alive and managed to sit up. Rabaut lay prostrate on the deck, Marie was scrambling hastily toward me, the men were running with wild cries. The foremast was in very mid-air, splintered, in the act of falling. It crashed down athwart the bows, and the lugger rocked and swayed like a small boat. Then Marie was at my side, flinging her arms around me, burying her face against my breast.

"I'm afraid—I'm afraid!" she cried out like a child, and clung to me, shaken with gasping breaths.

"The vengeance of St. Michael!" shrilled up a thin and panicky scream from one seaman's throat. Other men repeated it, hurled the words back and forth in stark mad fear. Somewhere forward showed a flicker of yellow light. "Afire—doomed!" rang out the yell. "Away from her—she is accursed, accursed!"

A frenzy of blind fear had gripped them all. In a moment these grown men had become worse than frightened children, blind to everything, impenetrable to all reason. They clustered about a small boat amidships and got it into the water.

In vain I shouted at them. Another levin-bolt ripped into the sea a quarter-mile away, with splitting crack and thunderous peal. It drew shrieks of mad terror from the men. Into the boat they tumbled, careless of provision or water; a rag of sail flew up, and out scurried the boat to leeward of us and away on the freshening breeze. So went the poor fools to their doom.

Up forward, the flicker of flame grew stronger. We were afire from the lightning.

"Marie, Marie!" I cried, shaking myself until the white face of the girl lifted and her eyes came to mine. "At my waist—my knife! Get it quickly, cut me free!"

A shudder passed through her body, then she seemed to realize the meaning of my words. Lifting herself, she searched until she came upon my long fisherman's knife and drew it out. I groaned despairingly as she fumbled for the cords about my wrists and hacked vainly at them—would she never manage it? Then, abruptly, my arms were free.

Not long enough tied up to have become numbed, I seized the knife from her hand, cut my feet loose and staggered up. The wind was increasing, but very gradually, the storm was still holding afar. Now and again thunderbolts hurtled into the sea or swept great gashes through the dark clouds, the peals and rumblings nearly continuous.

NOT EVEN SAINT MICHAEL

I ran forward, and there came stumbling to a halt in horrified realization of our actual plight. The whole bows of the ship were a mass of wreckage, and through this was spouting flame from the fore-castle hatch—a sheet of flame solid enough to show at one glance how helpless I was to cope with it.

Already it was catching the tarred rigging and canvas forward, the fallen spars, and spreading like wildfire. The bolt must have struck some stored oil or other inflammable material, perhaps spirits for smuggling. With one sudden rush, the licking blaze leaped twenty feet in air and spouted high.

Turning, I came back to Marie, who now stood leaning against the quarter-rail, her eyes on the flames. I halted before her with a helpless gesture.

"Your miracle was a trifle too strong for one dose," I shouted, to reach above the rattle of distant thunder. "The men have gone. We're afire and lost, between the blaze and the coming storm——"

"There were two boats!" she cried. "The other ——"

"Crushed under the fallen mast yonder. Call down another miracle, if you can," I added bitterly, "for we'll have full need of it."

She came a step closer to me, reached out and laid her hand on my arm. To my startled amazement I found her smiling. Then her voice came to me, clear and cool.

"Why doubt? Do you think it was not a miracle, indeed?"

I made an impatient gesture. "If you like. We're sadly in need of another——"

The words died on my lips. Marie's mouth fell open, she put a hand to her throat, her eyes drove past me and widened. I whirled, startled.

Rabaut was just coming to his feet.

CHAPTER XVI

IF A MIRACLE COULD BE EXPLAINED, IT WOULD BE
NONE

UNTIL this instant I had thought Rabaut
dead—had not even dared to look at
the charred and blackened figure.
Now I saw him unhurt, apparently. He moved
slowly and came erect, stood and looked around. In
his actions was a singular wooden stiffness, extremely unnatural. He seemed dazed, as well he
might, and yet something in his manner held me
spellbound, aghast, sent a chill down my back. The
snuffbox was still in his hand, and he sprang the
catch of it and took a pinch of the brown dust, as
though completing the act begun moments before.
It was all very mechanical, strangely done.

"A devilish smell of sulphur in the air," he said,
and looked at the two of us as though we were not
there. Something in his words, in their intonation,
in his whole air, raised the hair on my head with

a distinct prickle. "After all, my dear Michael," he went on, "I think you—you—you were a little hasty——"

His voice died away. He staggered, then suddenly collapsed into a limp heap and lay motionless. I went to him, lifted his head—he was quite dead. Also he was quite cold, as though he had been dead for long minutes.

Fear entered into me at this—fear I could not explain or put away. I straightened up, caught at the rail and stood trying to master myself. The feeling was on me that here I had heard a dead man speak, had seen a dead man move and act; impossible, incredible as it was, none the less this was my thought and fear.

I found Marie at my side and turned quickly to her, caught her hand, and held it for a long moment against my lips. Now I understood why she had flung herself upon me with her cry of childish terror—something of the same terror, though with less reason, was upon me. I looked into her eyes and tried to smile but failed. She read my fear, and her other hand came out to pat mine softly.

"Look! Look at me! Am I afraid any longer?" she said. I found her eyes very cool and darkly serene, and the smile on her lips was wistful.

IF A MIRACLE COULD BE EXPLAINED

"Don't laugh at miracles, but look up, over the rail —there——"

She turned me about and pointed. For a moment I could see nothing. The roar of the flames up forward and the rumbling of heaven's artillery filled my ears, the spouting red blaze was blinding to my eyes; then my vision cleared, and I beheld. Not a quarter-mile distant, speeding upon us out of the north under reefed canvas, was a ship.

Slowly the realization of it beat in upon me. She had seen us, was heading for the mounting beacon of flame, and would be under our stern in a scant few moments. I remembered now the rag of sail we had seen off to the north—how long ago? Half an hour perhaps, so swiftly had events moved, yet seemingly hours ago.

With a hoarse shout I broke into life, tore off my coat, waved it around my head. As though in response, an ensign was run up. The very sight of it brought a heart-leap in my throat.

"There's your miracle—look!" I caught Marie's arm. "My flag—an American sloop of war—she's heading for us——"

"Come, then," said Marie. "Help me."

I turned, found her trying to raise her brother, and bent to her aid. His eyes opened as we lifted him, and he put out one hand to the rail, staring around. Marie's eyes went to me, and she motioned forward, questioningly.

"There's time," she said. "The gold is there—you can reach it——"

My bare foot struck against something and I glanced down at the deck. Then I stooped and picked up her little wooden rosary and gave it to her.

"No," I said. "Let Rabaut keep his gold—or else the prior owner! I'll go to America with a greater treasure——"

Marie answered my smile, and the flames forward went roaring down the stiffening wind.

THE END